ONE SMALL STEP FOR MAN . . . ONE QUANTUM LEAP FOR MANKIND

Theorizing that a man could time travel within his own lifetime, Dr. Sam Beckett stepped into the Quantum Leap Accelerator—and vanished.

Somehow he was transported not only in time, but into *someone else's* life. . . .

And the Quantum Leap Project took on a whole new dimension.

QUANTUM LEAP

Now all the excitement and originality of the acclaimed television show are captured in these independent novels . . . all-new adventures, all-new leaps!

**OUT OF TIME. OUT OF BODY.
OUT OF CONTROL.**

QUANTUM LEAP

KNIGHTS OF THE MORNINGSTAR

A NOVEL BY

MELANIE RAWN

BASED ON THE UNIVERSAL TELEVISION
SERIES "QUANTUM LEAP"
CREATED BY DONALD P. BELLISARIO

ACE BOOKS, NEW YORK

Quantum Leap: Knights of the Morningstar, a novel by Melanie Rawn,
based on the Universal television series QUANTUM LEAP,
created by Donald P. Bellisario.

This book is an Ace original edition,
and has never been previously published.

QUANTUM LEAP: KNIGHTS OF THE MORNINGSTAR

An Ace Book / published by arrangement with
MCA Publishing Rights, a Division of MCA, Inc.

PRINTING HISTORY
Ace edition / September 1994

Copyright © 1994 by MCA Publishing Rights,
a Division of MCA, Inc. All rights reserved.
Cover art by Keith Birdsong.
This book may not be reproduced in whole or in part,
by mimeograph or any other means, without permission.
For information address: The Berkley Publishing Group,
200 Madison Avenue, New York, NY 10016.

ISBN: 0-441-00092-4

ACE®
Ace Books are published by The Berkley Publishing Group,
200 Madison Avenue, New York, NY 10016.
ACE and the "A" design are trademarks
belonging to Charter Communications, Inc.

PRINTED IN THE UNITED STATES OF AMERICA

10 9 8 7 6 5 4 3 2 1

For *QL* fans who, like me, refuse to believe
that Sam never returned home.
And for Scott Bakula and Dean Stockwell—
who made the series *so* easy on the eyes. . . .

AUTHOR'S NOTE

Although the terms "timeline" and "Quantum Leaping" are pretty much mutually exclusive, a word is necessary for continuity's sweet sake. This story takes place after "Deliver Us from Evil" and before "Return/Revenge."

QUANTUM LEAP

KNIGHTS OF THE MORNINGSTAR

PROLOGUE

Nervetingle—musclequiver—skinprickle—lightdazzle—synapses fieryhot—

No, that wasn't possible. Brainburn was not a hazard of his job.

But sometimes it sure felt like it.

As always, he tried to fix a memory in his mind. A single, simple thing: person, place, event, scent, touch. . . . Not that it ever did any good. People he'd helped, people he'd grown to care about, things he'd learned or done or prevented from happening—history as it had been and would not now be—in that familiar split instant of nothingness he sensed it all slip away.

He let it go.

And, for a fragment of Time, was himself. Displaced from one moment in the Past, suspended inside a single blink of the Present, he was himself again: whole and intact.

Samuel John Beckett. Born August 8, 1953, Elk Ridge, Indiana. Son of John Barrett and Thelma Katherine (nee Taylor) Beckett. Younger brother of

Thomas Edward, older brother of Katherine Louisa. Their faces before him, their voices resonating in his heart, brought memories of the tall green corn and the barn's warm redolence on cold January mornings.

He remembered.

He remembered the morning—he couldn't have been more than two—when Mom said Tom would be leaving for the day, gone at some place called secondgrade—Now don't take on so Sam it's all right just like Dad leaves every day (for another place called backforty) and *he* always comes home doesn't he? But he cried anyway, scared that Tom wouldn't come home.

He remembered another day when it snowed so much Tom couldn't go to secondgrade and Dad couldn't go to backforty, and how Tom got mad and then big-eyed when he caught Sam with the books Grandma Nettie sent for Christmas. A game of "What's That Word" quickly became "How Long Have You Been Reading" and then "Hey Mom Guess What." For a while everybody made kind of a big deal that he was only two and a half, but then things settled down and Grandma Nettie started sending *him* books, too.

He remembered a night in spring when thunder never stopped and lightning split the sky open and rain lashed the house all night long, and in the hall Dad said Damn it worst storm in a month of Sundays the road's flooded where's the doctor, and Tom came into his room and said Don't worry Sam it's just thunder Mom's gonna be fine the doctor will

2

come soon. The doctor *did* come, and so did the baby sister.

He remembered school: too smart for his own good, too shy for his own comfort. Skipping half a grade, then another, and suddenly too short for his own school yard safety (but there'd been only the one fight; Tom had made sure of that).

By high school he'd grown tall, and awkward with it. Tom suggested sports, and because Tom had played basketball so did he, training too-long legs and arms into submission (if not grace) on the court. Still too smart and too shy, but the girls began to look interested instead of scornful. He trained his treacherous voice, too, in the choir, and his hands at guitar and piano—he remembered her glorious smile as he played Chopin from memory, having seen the pages only once—

How much he could recall with that phenomenal photographic memory of his! And how it mocked him now.

He kept remembering while he still could, habitually greedy for information, knowing its play through his mind would not last.

College: Massachusetts Institute of Technology, B.S. and M.S. and Ph.D. in Physics so *fast*—and the other campuses, the other degrees, the M.D. from . . . from . . .

He couldn't remember.

No, not yet—please!

Stanford? Harvard? Johns Hopkins? UCLA? *Where?*

The memories were clouding now. So soon. Too soon.

3

School and study and exams and labs; papers and theses and doctoral dissertations—

Project Star Bright—

The Nobel prize—

There was more to him, there had to be. The sum of his life couldn't be nothing but an academic vita.

He began again (Samuel John Beckett, born August 8, 1953—) but the nearer Past was upon him now, demanding his mind. The Past he'd lived twice now, once for himself and once in bits and pieces of other people's lives.

He existed in a fragment of his own Time, his own identity. And both were changing as the changes he'd made changed *him*. Memories shifted as Time did its work on them, reflecting his work. The world swirled around him, a bright blue-white vortex centered on his stunned confusion—*had he truly done so much?* What he remembered spun and merged with what he also remembered: glimpses and impressions, enigmatically twinned, played out all around him. Separate truths and differing realities, superimposed one on the other, two images of each melding into a blur and then a resolution—

—a slim, dark-haired woman in a blood-spattered pink suit

—a girl of ten or twelve whose wise, beautiful eyes reminded him of Katie (but was there something of him in her face, too?)

—a proud old lady kneeling before her husband's grave

—another little girl, blaming herself for not being the son her grieving parents had lost

4

—a lovely young woman in the nurse's whites of the U.S. Navy, cradling a bouquet of calla lilies in her arms

—an old man with falcon's eyes, determined to die on the land of his ancestors

His mind tried to catalog them, make sense and order. His heart cried out to know, to be certain that what had happened was right, that the changes had been for the better.

Peace, Dr. Beckett. All is as it should be.

The bright whirlwind steadied and his questions stilled. All except one. If everything was as it was supposed to be, then—

Not yet. Home is waiting for you. But not yet.

Rebellion flared. WHEN? he cried silently.

There was no answer. There never was. Perhaps there never would be.

His life slipped away from him then, the rainbow dance of memories engulfed in a blaze of purest light. All the faces, the names, the feelings, the deeds— even his own name—vanished.

He let it go.

And, as always, he hung on to one word. Mantra, focus, summation of all that was important to him— of all that he truly was.

Home. . . .

Time and reality coalesced again. His body and brain stopped ringing.

And he felt his right arm sag with the weight of something heavy gripped in his fingers. He blinked, and shifted his shoulders, and lifted his hand.

The arm wore gleaming chain mail. The hand

wore a battered leather gauntlet. The fingers held a long, shining sword.

He heard a thunk that could have been his jaw dropping. He looked down. From its place propped between his elbow and hip, a silvery helmet sporting a green plume had fallen to the ground.

The sword sank again to his side. Disappointment (not home, not by a long shot) was swept away in a flash flood of intense curiosity and equally intense confusion. *When? Where? Who? Why?* Strongest of all was the urgent need to do and say the right things—or at least to avoid the wrong things until those four essential questions were answered.

When was usually the toughest, so he deferred it. (Besides, he didn't much like the implications of that chain mail.) *Where* was usually the easiest; all he need do was look. So he did.

And gulped.

All around him was a sylvan glade awash in summer sunshine and medieval splendor. Multicolored pennants, some plain and some bearing coat of arms, fluttered in a warm breeze. Jugglers in court-jester outfits and minstrels in motley, ladies fair in flowing garb, roving merchants hawking their wares, squires carrying swords and shields, knights in chain mail— the whole woodland scene positively reeked chivalric panoply circa 1450 or so. The only thing missing was a castle atop a hill.

He flinched as a roar sounded from somewhere beyond the screening trees. Cheers and applause— at least he hadn't Leaped into the middle of a battle, he thought with relief, and instantly felt like a fool. Did any of these people look worried? They were having a great time—all except for the guy crouched over there cranking a rotisserie, on which what looked like an entire cow revolved slowly over the fire pit.

The sensation of idiocy increased as he heard several metallic crashes behind him. Turning, he beheld a hewn-log sawhorse against which shields, swords, and lances had been propped until his startled reaction to the cheers had knocked them over.

He busied himself picking them up. They clattered again when someone yelled, "Sir Percival? Sir Percival of York!"

Sam had the uncanny—and sinking—feeling that Sir Percival was none other than him.

A herald advanced on Sam. A herald he could only be: rolled-up scrolls protruded like wayward feathers from his purple tunic, a brass hunting horn dangled from his belt, and a golden crown badge of royal service was stitched on his velvet-covered chest.

"Sir Percival! You joust next against Lord Rannulf." The herald pointed.

Nearby, a knight warmed up his fighting muscles by taking swipes at the air with his sword. Lord Rannulf was six feet four inches and 225 pounds of solid sinew in glinting chain mail. Conan the Antiquarian. He looked able to crush skulls singlehandedly.

A mighty swing of the blade turned him in Sam's direction. Their gazes met. His lordship grinned.

All Sam could manage was a feeble, "Oh, boy."

CHAPTER
ONE

You know, I was starting to think I'd done it all. Well, most of it, anyway. I could remember being a lounge singer, a Mafia hitman, a Southern lawyer, a talk-show host, a cop—several times, I think—and I've even been pregnant. Sort of.

But never, ever, had I Leaped into a fifteenth century chain-link mosquito net.

Now, it couldn't be the real *fifteenth century. I mean, I can only Leap within my own lifetime, right?*

Boy, do I hope *I can only Leap within my own lifetime. Because this sure* looks *like the fifteenth century.*

"Sir Percival?" the herald said. "You're ready for the joust?"

"Uh—" With that Matterhorn of medieval musculature? Sam gulped again. "I, uh—"

Unperturbed by ineloquent monosyllables—which probably meant "Sir Percival" was usually as tongue-tied as Sam was right now—the herald nodded and darted away, calling for somebody named Lord Godwyn. Sam dragged his gaze from the hulking

Lord Rannulf and crouched to pick up his plumed helmet.

Three feet away there suddenly appeared a pair of dainty hand-stitched leather slippers. Sam straightened slowly. Above the slippers was a hint of slim ankles in yellow hose. The rest of both legs was hidden by a wide red skirt. This narrowed to an intricately tooled leather belt from which hung a velvet drawstring purse and a sheathed dagger with a bright green stone in the hilt. Above all this was a yellow laced bodice—out of which generous portions of the lady's anatomy were in imminent danger of spilling.

Sam finally met the girl's eyes: leaf-green below curling brown hair topped by a perky white cap. She was smiling at him. One of the long-lashed eyes winked.

"Ho, Sir Knight! A bracing cup before your joust?" She held out a lidded pewter stein of heroic proportions—say, half a gallon or so. Her accent, Sam noted absently, was Irish. More or less.

Juggling sword and helm, he ended by dropping both. Again. Either he'd reverted to his adolescent clumsiness around pretty girls, or Sir Percival was not only inarticulate but so seriously klutzy that it dominated the Leap. And if the latter were the case, he'd be in even worse trouble against Lord Rannulf.

Worse? The sword weighed a ton and he didn't have a clue how to use it. *Worse* did not apply.

Aware that the girl expected an answer, he mumbled, "Uh—no, no thanks—"

"It's a clear head ye'll be wantin', then? For mesel', Sir Knight, I'd take a good long swig first, to dull the pain!" She gestured to Lord Rannulf, who was still slicing up the inoffensive breeze. "Well, here's to hopin' ye'll be alive to drink it after! He looks in fine fettle this tourney morn!"

Didn't he just. Sam hid a wince, picturing his neck in the pathway of three feet of gleaming steel. The image thus evoked was not comforting.

With another wink, the girl sauntered off. Sam collected sword and helmet once more from the grass. As he turned, the rack of polished shields and other items of medieval mayhem caught the sunlight—and his convexity-warped reflection.

Sir Percival was about Sam's own height and at least twenty pounds skinnier. A thirtysomething scholarly type, he looked as if he should be wearing a pocket protector, not chain mail. His hairline was receding a trifle (maybe that was the effect of the shield's curvature, but Sam doubted it) into nondescript mousy waves that needed a trim, and the dominant feature of his long-jawed face was a nose only a rhino might envy. Saving Sir Percy from terminal nerdship were his remarkably fine eyes, an unusual shade of hazel sparked with green and gold, shaded by thick, blunt lashes.

Still, he was hardly the image of the daring knight-errant.

A loud *whoosh* nearby spun Sam around. Al had arrived—half in and half out of a tree trunk.

"About time you got here," Sam hissed. Then he looked again. "What in the name of Giorgio Armani have you got on?"

Rather than the dress whites and fruit salad of a Rear Admiral, United States Navy, Alberto Ernesto

Giovanni-Battista Calavicci wore a suit whose colors were strongly reminiscent of the fruit salad crowning Carmen Miranda. Lemon satin trousers. Concord grape shirt. Tangerine jacket with lime lapels. Raspberry tie. Orange loafers.

Sam shook his head in honest amazement. The man had no shame. And no taste, either.

Al was paying him not the slightest heed. Gleaming brown eyes round as saucers, he was surveying the scene with an expression of utter bliss. Even the smoke from his cigar seemed to curl with particular glee.

Sam retreated behind the oak as a pair of jugglers passed by, jingling with bells and dressed in green and orange checks that made Al look almost conservative.

"Al? Where—no, *when* am I? Al!"

"Mmm?"

"Damn it, get out of that tree and talk to me!"

"What? Oh." He obligingly stepped forward. Sam almost wished he'd stayed in the tree—the left sleeve of the tangerine jacket ended in a banana-colored cuff.

"You're at a medieval tournament, of course. Sam, isn't this incredible? Like a book of fairy tales come to life!" He was eating this up with a spoon. Another minute and he'd start to declaim *Idylls of the King*.

"A medieval—? I can't Leap centuries." He felt a twinge of panic. "*Tell* me I can't Leap centuries—"

Still not listening. "Y'know, when I was a kid, my buddies and I were all the knights of the Round Table. Gawain, Galahad, Lancelot. . . . These kids

11

with their computer games, they miss all the real fun. We used to lay siege to fortresses—well, really the attic at the orphanage, but with a little imagination it was pretty impressive. There were running sword fights on the stairs, dragons to slay in the garage, fair maidens to be rescued from fiendish wizards—"

Right on cue, the green-eyed wench sashayed by again, toasting Sam with the pewter mug. Al leered wistfully.

"Al." Sam waved the sword in his partner's face. Had Al not been a hologram, he would have needed corrective rhinoplasty. "Talk to me. Tell me what's going on."

The girl was followed by the herald. "Sir Percival of York, to joust against Lord Rannulf of the Franks!"

After a fulminating glare for Al—who didn't notice, still enchanted by this evocation of childhood fantasies—Sam stepped from behind the tree. He trudged along behind the herald to a fenced clearing the size of a soccer field. At one end was a raised dais flanked by tiered benches, overhung with a purple canvas canopy against the sun. At least a hundred men, women, and children in lavish medieval dress thronged the seats around two large chairs, on which sat a crowned couple. Lord Rannulf was in the process of bowing to them. Managing a sickly smile, Sam followed suit.

The herald cleared his throat importantly. "If it please Your Majesties, the joust of knightly skill between Lord Rannulf of the Franks and Sir Percival of York will now commence!"

12

Knightly skill? Sam thought wildly. *Does that mean he's not gonna try to skewer me?*

The queen—a charming, sweet-faced Chinese lady of about forty wearing a purple gown and a silver circlet to hold her wimple in place—leaned forward. "Good fortune to you both, my lord, Sir Knight."

"I thank Your Majesty," said Lord Rannulf.

Feeling that some equally courtly response was called for, Sam added, "Your Majesty is most gracious."

The royal couple beamed. The crowd applauded. The herald backed off. And Sam prepared himself for a walloping.

But Lord Rannulf's attention was now directed at a wimpled and dimpled damsel seated on a bench near the queen. The lady was perhaps thirty, pleasantly rounded, and very pretty in a girl-next-manor sort of way. Blond curls escaped the wimple to wisp her forehead above blue eyes and soft cheeks that blushed a few shades darker than her helpless silken flutter of a petal-pink gown.

Lord Rannulf swept her a low bow. "I beg a token, sweet lady, to carry me through to victory."

The lady looked at Sam.

Significantly.

Total bafflement during the first hours of a Leap was not unusual, especially when Al was being no help at all. Sam stood there exhibiting all the intelligent comprehension of a potted plant. It was a painfully familiar sensation.

The lady, obviously disappointed by Sam's lack of response, glanced away. After a moment she tossed

13

Lord Rannulf the white scarf draping her shoulders. He placed it briefly to his lips—the crowd went wild—and tied it around his upper left arm. One last bow, and he started for the center of the tourney field. It was all very nicely done, exactly according to the Chivalric Rule Book, and made Sam feel like an uncouth lout.

He might have minded less if he'd felt like an uncouth lout who knew what the hell was going on.

Glumly, he followed Lord Rannulf. The sight of massive shoulders, swathed in chain mail and about four feet wide, did nothing for his self-confidence. Surreptitiously he tested the edge of his sword. Not only did he not slice off a finger, the blade didn't even put a scratch in the leather gauntlet.

"Keep your guard up," said a familiar voice beside him as he walked. "And remember, this sword's the real thing and a lot heavier than that stage prop you waved around when you did *Man of La Mancha*—"

Sam really, truly, seriously hated it when Al made references that made no sense. "When I did *what*?"

"Never mind. Put your helmet on, Sir Percy."

Sam crammed seven pounds of metal over his ears. The chafe against his brow told him why Sir Percival was going bald. As he turned his head, a slotted visor flipped down with a clank to cover his face, startling him.

"I can't see a thing in this helmet. How am I supposed to fight? And this sword wouldn't cut butter."

"Did you think you were in the *real* fifteenth century?"

14

He was abruptly glad of the visor; it hid the hot flush in his cheeks.

Al chortled. "You *did*! You thought this was for real!"

"Did not," Sam muttered.

"Did so!"

"Did *not*!"

"Ha! Ziggy's gonna love this!"

"Well, let's see Ziggy stand here in a steel oven while Lord Rannulf over there makes her into shish kebab!"

"Oh, chill out. You heard the herald. Jousts are to demonstrate skill, not to draw blood. All the weapons are blunted."

Lord Rannulf was stretching his muscles. One more flex, and he'd burst his chain mail.

"Imagine my relief," said Sam.

"The sword's authentic enough," Al went on. "It's just not sharp. The point is, do you know how to use it?"

The royal herald forced a massive note from his brass hunting horn, proving that lung capacity was a prerequisite of the job. Lord Rannulf responded to the signal and came at Sam like a Sherman tank with a sword where the cannon should have been. Sam didn't have a prayer; all he managed was a lot of flailing around as he tried to keep his skin and Lord Rannulf's sword as unacquainted as possible.

"Guess not," Al remarked.

"Come on, show me your stuff!" his lordship taunted.

"There's a balance to a fine sword, Sam—get the feel of it, use the momentum—"

"You look like you practice by slicing sausage!"

"Come on, Sam, get him!"

Every so often Sam held an idle debate with himself about which was the single most irritating thing about Quantum Leaping. Those first minutes or hours of uncertainty? Coaxing even semi-accurate projections out of a temperamental computer? Coaxing answers out of a hot-tempered Italian-American admiral? Trying to remember that he must answer to a name not his own? Easy stuff, compared to what he now decided once and for all was the most infuriating aspect of this insanity he was caught up in: sorting out two conversations at once.

One of these two loudmouths was going to have to shut up or Sam was going to blow a gasket.

He took a swing at Lord Rannulf. Al moaned in despair. "It's not a tennis racket, Sam!"

"Or maybe taking slices with a golf club?" suggested his lordship, with a swipe that neatly mimicked Sam's graceless move. Unlike Sam, however, he very nearly connected. "Fore!"

"Lean into it, Sam! Block him!"

Hot, sweating, and increasingly frustrated, Sam blocked the next swing at the last second, then surged in as he'd seen fencers do. But they used sabers or foils or thin little rapiers or whatever they called them; this thing, however balanced and blunted, weighed at least ten pounds. What took an Olympic fencer a flick of one supple wrist required both Sam's arms up to the shoulders and most of the muscles of his back. He was in good shape, but sword muscles were specialized and he was pulling all the wrong ones. He was sweating like a plow horse, his hair was plastered to his forehead under the heavy steel helm, his left bicep ached where Lord Rannulf had gotten in a good thwack, and the mail grated against his neck where shirt and quilted padding had shifted down.

Sam Beckett was not a happy camper.

"Aw, Sam, show a little finesse!"

Lord Rannulf was showing off now, swinging his sword one-handed, waving Sam closer with his free hand. Laughter echoed tinnily from inside his helmet. More casual, contemptuous slices of silver; more advice from Al the Kibitzing Hologram; more sweat running down his forehead to sting his eyes; more outraged protests from his back muscles.

"Throw your weight forward, Sam, get under his guard—no, not like that! It's a sword, not a toilet plunger!"

That's it, Sam thought. *That is absolutely IT!*

"If you don't shut up—" he yelled, threatening a swing at Al.

Being a hologram, Al was profoundly unimpressed. But Lord Rannulf took the opportunity to deal Sam a resounding slap across the chest with the flat of his sword that made every link of mail shiver.

"Home run!" his lordship crowed.

Sam landed on his backside in soft, sweet-smelling summer grass. Unhappily, just below that grass was hard, dry summer ground. He hurt all the way to his hair.

Lord Rannulf stood over him to his left; to his right stood Al. Both were shaking their heads—and definitely not in amazement at Sam's prowess.

17

Rannulf eased out of his helmet and grinned.

"Nice move. You'll have to teach me that one. Bet it thrilled Cynthia right down to her toes." He swept Sam a mocking bow and headed for the royal dais to receive his accolade.

Exhausted, and considerably less than thrilled himself, Sam pushed back his visor and glared up at Al.

"Pathetic," the admiral announced in disgust. "Just pathetic. Didn't you ever play Rescue the Maiden when you were a kid? Capture the Castle? Pirate Ships? No, probably not. Too busy memorizing logarithms."

Sam, still on his butt, pointed the sword directly at the knot of Al's raspberry silk tie. "Just tell me why that goon in shining armor is trying to kill me. Would you do me that one little favor? Please?"

With a snort and a smirk, Al punched buttons on the handlink. "Come on, Sir Percy. Let's go back to your tent. You don't look so good."

CHAPTER TWO

Not that Sam had any notion where the tent was. He merely limped along through the campground behind Al, who seemed to know perfectly well where he was going. After all, Al had Ziggy.

What Sam had was a sore back, an even sorer backside, a nape chafed raw, two aching arms, and a powerful need for a long, hot bath. The tent Al waved him into promised nothing more therapeutic than an aspirin.

Still, the modernity of the big khaki-colored White Stag was a relief. Not that he'd *really* believed he was *really* in the fifteenth century. . . . And if he had, he'd never admit it.

Sir Percival's tent was a miracle of luxury compared to some of the others set up in the wooded campground. Vintage WWI pup tents and cramped little domes abounded, and there were even a few tarp canopies slung casually from poles with snarls of blankets inside for bedding. Sam appreciated Sir Percy even more when he got inside. The man had a nice eye to his own comfort, even while living out his medieval dreams.

The folding camp bed was made up with sheets and pillows instead of a sleeping bag. A Coleman lantern hung from the central tent pole. A sponge floated in a bucket of clean water that Sam was tempted to dump over his head. But that would probably rust the chain mail with him in it. Visions of the Tin Man came to mind, but the lyric in his head belonged to the Scarecrow: *"If I only had a brain . . ."*

A wooden coat tree stood sentinel in the corner near a folding chair with clean clothes piled neatly on the seat. Another chair was shoved beneath a collapsible table, on which rested shaving kit, first-aid box (Sam lunged for the aspirin bottle), and a boom box with a case of cassettes. He slipped the pills down his throat and swallowed them dry, then slid a tape of Celtic harp music into the cassette player just in case somebody happened along outside while he was talking with Al. Then he squatted down to get at the ice chest.

The chain mail chimed charmingly, percussion provided by the crack of Sam's left knee and right shoulder bones. He rubbed the small of his back and straightened up again. First order of business was this miserable metal prison. He began what proved to be a protracted struggle with it while Al punched the handlink into submission and relayed Ziggy's latest news flash.

"It's Saturday, July 11, 1987, and you're at a weekend tournament held by the Medieval Chivalry League. Six times a year they get together in costume to relive the glory and romance of the past."

He struck a noble pose, as if for a heroic sculpture. He looked more like a lawn jockey. "In days of old, when men were bold, and knighthood was in flower—"

Sam grunted, wrenching more muscles as he battled the mail shirt. The thing came down to his knees, split front and back to the crotch—presumably for ease of horseback riding, though he'd neither seen nor smelled horses around here. Small favors. "Doesn't this thing have a zipper?"

Al was shocked at the very idea. "Costumes and armor are strictly authentic at League functions!"

"Authentic. Wonderful. Is there an authentic way out of this?"

The Sir Lancelot wanna-be considered. "Maybe if you work it both sleeves at a time, like a sweater."

He couldn't have been less helpful even if he hadn't been a hologram. The suggested maneuver put Sam in immediate peril of strangulation.

"Well, try hiking it up over your butt, and then you can sit down, and—"

"Just tell me the who and what and why, okay?" Sam interrupted from somewhere inside twenty pounds of woven steel.

"My, my. Testy, aren't we? Your League name is Sir Percival of York—*New* York, that is. Manhattan's about ninety minutes thataway." He waved the cigar vaguely. "The fair maiden is Lady Cyndaria of the Chimes—also known as Cynthia Mulloy, fiction editor at a New York publishing house."

"Lady Who of What?"

"Pay attention, Sam. You'll have to call these people by their League titles. They're very strict about not using 'mundane' names. You're Sir Percival of

21

York, she's Lady Cyndaria of the Chimes. Got it?"

"Yeah, yeah. I got it." He'd also gotten most of the mail up around his shoulders. Hefting with both hands, he pushed it over his head and jumped to one side. It clinked and rattled to the floor, and lay like like an unstuffed metallic scarecrow.

"Be careful!" Al admonished. "You'll twist the links all out of shape. Somebody put a lot of work into making that, y'know."

"Slaving all day over a hot forge?" Sam rubbed his neck gingerly. "Come on, Al."

"You think you can pick up one of these things wholesale at Helmets 'R' Us? I told you, Sam, everyone here wears authentic period costumes. Not only do they not allow zippers, they can't even use sewing machines. Now, put that on the rack over there, with the helmet."

Sam dutifully did as told. "You sound like my mother. 'Pick up your clothes, Sam!'"

Al grinned. "I kinda doubt she ever had to tell you to hang up your chain mail. You know how they used to clean it, back in the olden days? They'd sew it into a leather sack filled with sand to scrape the rust off, and give it to the squires to toss around—like football practice."

Sam chuckled at the idea of throwing a Hail Mary pass that weighed twenty pounds. He lost his smile when he saw the lacings of his padded tunic. There were at least two dozen of them, located down his right side and knotted so tightly he was tempted to break them. But he forbore; he didn't want to wreck Sir Percy's property, considering he was probably here to salvage the wreck of Sir Percy's life.

22

Probably. Maybe. It occurred to him then that Al was taking a long time to get to the point.

"So why am I here? To keep Cynthia—excuse me, Lady Cyndaria—from buying a lousy manuscript?"

"No, smart guy. In fact, this coming Monday morning she draws up the contract for the best-seller that makes her career. Ziggy thinks she must've read the manuscript this weekend."

Sam nodded and draped the quilted tunic over the chain mail. Shirt next: fine white linen, limp with sweat, sporting about a hundred more little laces down the front. Zippers he was willing to concede— but hadn't they known about buttons in 1450?

"If it's not Cynthia, then what?"

Al said exactly nothing.

Fingers pausing on a knot, Sam regarded his friend. Long practice in reading that expressive face—especially when it was, as now, carefully expressionless—alerted him. Al wasn't telling. Not yet. And trying to force it out of him was, as Sam well knew, practically impossible. He'd tell it in his own way, in his own time. But the look in his dark eyes made the fine hairs on Sam's nape itch.

"Lord Rannulf," Al resumed, "the guy who just basted you with a sword, his real name is Roger Franks. He won his League title with his skill in jousting. So did our good Sir Percy, by the way— and I gotta tell ya, Sam, you didn't do his reputation much good today." He clucked his tongue against his teeth. "In the first place, you don't hold a sword like it's a chicken and you're trying to wring its neck. In the second place—"

"Lecture me later," Sam interrupted. "Just tell me—"

"Why you're here. Okay. Well, first of all, there's Cynthia. She makes stained-glass wind chimes, by the way. Thus the name. You earn rank by skill in crafts or jousting or music, and at every League meeting there's the chance to earn points toward a knighthood or earldom or whatever."

Al was stalling. Sam, worrying his lower lip with his teeth as he worried another knot loose with his fingers, was very close to accusing him of willfully withholding information. But Al usually had very good reasons for drawing out the inevitable. So Sam merely asked, "You never said what Roger does in 'mundane' life. Bouncer in a medieval biker bar?"

"Cute. No, he's a researcher in parties—parties?" A slap to the handlink produced a squeal of electronic outrage. "Oh. *Particle.* Researcher in particle physics." He regarded Sam through a haze of mercifully illusory cigar smoke. If it was one thing Sam recalled about life B.Q.L. (Before Quantum Leaping), it was that Al smoked seriously stinky cigars.

"Don't you want to know who *you* are, Sam?"

Amazing. After ten minutes of evasion, Al was implying that *Sam* was the reluctant one? Someday, Sam vowed, someday when he was back home, Al was going to pay big-time for every single one of these annoyances.

Someday. *This* day, this moment, Sam saw a punch line coming. He was positive he wasn't going to find it funny at all.

"Philip Larkin," said Al.

The remaining laces ripped with the violence of

Sam's reaction. He yanked his way out of the shirt and threw it onto the camp cot. "Larkin? The 'Larkin Capacitor' Larkin?"

"That's you. Him. You remember?"

How he'd come to hate that question. Did he remember family, friends, events, songs, equations, String Theory—some or all of what he knew might or might not be available to him during any given Leap. One day he spoke fluent Spanish, but the next he didn't know how to say *buenos días*; one day he was a gifted physician, but the next he couldn't clip a hangnail without risking gangrene. He'd developed a philosophical streak about it that eased the frustration most of the time. What he truly needed to know, he was usually allowed to remember.

And Philip Larkin's name was lit up in his mind like a billboard on Sunset Strip.

"I remember what it cost to buy the rights to use the thing! But we had to have it. The man was an engineering wizard and the Capacitor solved all kinds of problems—" *What* kinds, he wasn't sure. Something to do with energy flow, maybe. But he did know that without the Larkin Capacitor, Project Quantum Leap would have taken several more years to complete.

Belatedly, he heard the past tense in reference to Larkin, and remembered something else. "I never met him. He died before I even found out about his invention."

Al nodded. "October, 1989."

"That's right."

"If you know so much," Al complained, "how come

you need me and Ziggy? Tell me about the Larkin Capacitor, genius."

The words came automatically to his lips—for about ten seconds. "A self-contained independent component attached to the Accelerator framework that regulates and modifies the necessarily intermittent and irregular flow of energy from . . . from . . ."

He knew Philip Larkin's name, and what he had devised, and how much of their hard-won funding it had taken to purchase the patented contraption from his estate—but not how it fit into the Quantum Leap Accelerator.

What Sam would have termed a frown of concentration, Al evidently saw as a grimace of singular ferocity. He raised both hands defensively.

"Hey, don't look at me! You and Larkin were the only ones who ever understood the gadget." An electronic whine made him wince, and there was a brief pause for the customary physical abuse of the handlink. "Yes, Ziggy. I hear you, Ziggy. Right away, Ziggy." He sighed. "She nags worse than my fourth wife—except I can't divorce her. She wants me to tell you that the Larkin Capacitor might be one of the glitches. It might be one reason we can't control your Leaps."

Sam began to pace, then caught himself at it and sat on the cot. "And for all I remember about how the Capacitor works—"

"That's my best buddy," Al interjected. "Nobel prize in physics and a mind like a steel sieve."

For all I know," he repeated irritably, "the blue wire might get plugged into the green socket or get wrapped around a Christmas tree. But if the

Capacitor's what went wrong, and it gets fixed—"

Something began to bubble inside him—wonderful, scary, crazy, full of hope and yelling a warning. Sam took a deep, steadying breath and fisted his hands on his knees to keep them from shaking.

"Is Larkin there? In the Waiting Room?"

"Yes, he's there—I mean here. Where else would he be?"

He could sit still no longer. Springing to his feet, he tried not to yell as he pointed out the obvious. "He invented the damned thing, didn't he? So he can fix it!"

Al frowned. "He's not in such good shape, Sam. Some people don't react well to the transfer—"

"Well, wake him up! Calm him down! Give him coffee, a brandy, sedatives—give him a good swift kick in the butt if you have to! Just get him to work on it!"

"There might be another way. Larkin patented his gizmo in 1989—after working on it for four years."

Sam knew that tone. It was the I've-just-said-something-extremely-significant tone Al used when Sam was supposed to draw his own conclusions. It took a moment, but Sam finally took the hint and started searching the tent. The cot, the sheets, the pillows; the table, the cassette case; the duffel bag of clothes in the corner; the briefcase under the table. . . .

He stopped cold. A battered leather briefcase leaned against a table leg just to one side of the ice chest. Slowly, in a hushed voice that vibrated with the pounding of his heart, he said, "Al . . . it's like when I went back to the farm that time . . . when

27

I saw my family again . . . I remember that Leap. It was for me. So is this. Al, this time it's for *me*. . . ."

Al was shaking his head solemnly. "No, Sam."

"How can you say that?" he demanded. "You don't know that!"

"I *do* know it. My God, nobody knows it better than I do!"

Sam turned away. "I don't want to hear about it."

"And if you don't remember, I'm not going to tell you. We've had this conversation before—whether you remember it or not! Ziggy says—"

"And don't quote me any damned odds from Ziggy! I know why I'm here, Al. I *know* it!"

"If I've learned nothing else since this started," Al went on with terrible intensity, "it's that no Leap is ever about our own lives. Even if we want it to be. It just doesn't work that way."

Another reminder that Al knew things Sam didn't. Al remembered all the Leaps. All the details. Sam retained only bits and pieces, like souvenirs he didn't recall buying in places he didn't remember visiting on vacations he wasn't sure he'd taken. All he really had were his instincts. And right now they were howling at him.

He saw his hands reach for the briefcase as if it were the Holy Grail. Which, for him, it might very well be.

"I *know* it," he repeated, stubborn and scared. "Even if *I* don't understand his notes, you can relay them to Ziggy through the handlink. She can work on them, and maybe—"

"Oh, Sam. Don't do this to yourself."

"Maybe I could get back home."

CHAPTER THREE

Roger Franks didn't particularly like particles, in physics or otherwise. He preferred a grander scale of things. The Big Picture. The bigger and grander the better, in fact. That was why he was Lord Rannulf of *all* the Franks, not just those in a village in Normandy to which he really had traced his ancestors, giving him one of the few genuine pedigrees in the League.

Happily encased in chain mail and his alter ego, he clung tightly to his token of victory. It was nothing more grand than a small round disk of beaten tin, but it would join the others on what His Majesty King Steffan I (who was part Cherokee) irreverently termed a "scalp belt." This item, a leather strip to which the disks were tied with thongs, was displayed outside Roger's tent. Societies similar to the Medieval Chivalry League had other rules and tokens of advancement in the nobility, but Roger preferred the solid feel of palm-sized circles of metal. Threading each new souvenir of his prowess onto his collection was his proudest task after each tourney. Eventually there would be enough for a dukedom, and in a couple of years he'd be eligible for election to the kingship.

At his side now walked the only woman he would accept as his queen.

Cynthia looked the perfect evocation of a medieval damsel: clothed with both modesty and elegance, blond as sunshine beneath her wimple, and winsomely lovely. He preened inwardly as they strolled, knowing they were the focus of all eyes, authentic enough to have stepped right from an illuminated manuscript or a cathedral window. Sword at his hip, helm dangling casually from his fingers, he was the very portrait of a noble knight escorting his lady fair from the tourney field. And she *was* his lady, at least for the rest of the evening. Her scarf, still knotted around his upper arm, proclaimed it for all to see. The breeze toyed with the silk, a wisp of incongruous femininity snagging on formidable chain mail.

"You were lucky today," Cynthia observed. "Sir Percival's not usually so easy a joust."

"Off his form, I guess." Roger shrugged, knowing she was right. Accounting for Phil's worse than amateurish fighting was not his main concern right now, though. "My lady, may I make so bold as to come by your tent later? After I clean off this dirt, of course."

"Lord Rannulf!" She batted long lashes at him, playful and sarcastic all at once. He enjoyed the former, wishing it wasn't accompanied by the latter. A real medieval lady would not be so . . . *forward*.

"My lord, you know very well what Queen Elinor said last spring when all the knights went skinny-dipping in the creek!" She pronounced it *crick*, thus betraying her Wyoming origins: small-town girl from Big Sky country with an English Lit. degree from Oberlin College, working her way to a senior editorship in the New York publishing world. The small mannerism of speech spoiled the medieval illusion; Roger determinedly put it out of his mind.

"I *still* say it's a total waste of League funds to rent portable showers," he grumbled. "This park has a perfectly good stream to bathe in. And it's more authentic, too. Hip baths would be acceptable, but those showers—"

"Now, I didn't say that our gracious sovereign minded for herself," Cynthia went on archly. "In fact, I think she was very upset when the local Smokey the Bear contingent happened by and spoiled her view."

A real medieval lady would *definitely* refrain from such suggestive comments. Roger very nearly blushed, and to cover it raked his fingers through his sweaty hair. He loved a good workout at the jousts, but the July sun made his armor an oven.

Cynthia pulled a face as his arm raised. "Your lordship, you stink. Swallow your objections and go take a shower. You may come by my tent only if you're clean—and only if you bring the famous manuscript with you."

This was what he'd been angling for, but now that she'd taken the bait he was strangely reluctant to start reeling in.

"Well . . . nobody's read it yet. I kind of wanted to get a first reaction from somebody other than an important editor."

"Editor, yes. Important—I'm working on it."

She winked at him, *lashes sweeping graceful as a bird's wing down over a lapis-blue eye. . . .* His literary instincts provided the description and filed it for future reference. Cynthia Mulloy was nothing if not inspirational.

"Oh, come on," she coaxed. "You've been hinting around for months! If you're serious about getting published, you really ought to have a professional give it a once-over."

Still he balked. "I'm not even sure if all the commas are in the right places."

Her sigh was a miracle of tolerance. "I promise I won't give it back to you bleeding red ink."

"Well . . ."

"Well?" she prompted.

"If you really think so."

"I really think so." When she laughed—*a sound as sweetly melodious as the wind-borne singing of her chimes*, he composed in his mind—she became Lady Cyndaria again, and he was enchanted. "Come, Lord Rannulf, this coy hesitation becomes you not! Courage!"

He bowed as extravagantly as to the Queen of France. Cynthia swept him a curtsy in reply, wimple fluttering delicately on the summer breeze, and his transportation back to the Middle Ages was complete. His soul swelled with it.

"By your leave, gentle lady," Roger intoned, rolling the words with a hint of the French accent he sometimes used. "I shall obey your every word without hesitation."

"Forward, my lord! Forward!"

32

She shattered the illusion once more by giving him a push. But he didn't mind. As she strolled off to her tent, the mighty Lord Rannulf of the Franks had a very hard time restraining a whoop of sheer glee.

Philip Larkin's briefcase contained the current issues of ten different technical journals, phone bills, computer brochures, a photocopied article on the Battle of Crécy, an elaborate spurious genealogy for Sir Percival of York, a garishly colored coat of arms for same, and similar frustrating and useless effluvia.

"I was pretty sure you'd remember Philip Larkin's name," Al was saying. "But you don't know who Roger is, do you?"

A scribbled page of notes turned out to be a grocery list. Sam snarled and kept searching. "I bet you're going to tell me."

"Roger Franks wrote the raciest, sexiest, juiciest, spiciest, *trashiest* best-seller of 1989. *Knights of the Morningstar*—that's knight with a K. Sold a gazillion copies. The movie was so hot they had to issue fire extinguishers with the tickets."

Sam gave a snort. "Roger doesn't look as if he could write a letter. Besides, what's a researcher in particle physics—*ha!*—doing writing a bodice ripper?"

"How should I know? And it's not just a bodice ripper. I mean, it's steamy stuff, but scholarly, too. The reviewers said everything was meticulously researched and you could get a pretty good education about the Crusades and life in medieval

33

France from reading Roger's book."

"The Middle Ages," Sam said wryly. "Otherwise known as 'a thousand years without a bath.'"

"They were probably a lot cleaner than you are right now. Boy, am I glad you're a hologram. You must smell like a stable."

Sam took an experimental sniff. Al was right. Did they take showers in the fifteenth century? Well, this was a state park campground, they ought to have showers someplace. And the idea of gallons of hot water beating down on his aching shoulders was sheer bliss.

"Roger also made pots of money and married his editor."

There it was—*that tone* again. Sam decided to ignore it, and Al, in favor of the briefcase.

"His editor was a certain blue-eyed blonde."

"Uh-huh."

"Who also belonged to the Medieval Chivalry League."

"Mmm-hmm."

"He married Cynthia, you twit!"

Sam flipped through a copy of the League newsletter. "I hope they're very happy."

"She divorced him after Philip died."

This snagged Sam's notice. "Huh?"

Center of attention once again, as was his just and proper due, Al took a luxurious pull at his cigar before continuing. "When she married Roger, Philip buried himself in his research. You know the type—all work, no fun—sound familiar?"

Pointedly: "No."

"Huh."

After a moment's rumination, Sam asked, "How did Philip die?"

"Well, after he left the League he took up a different hobby. Drinking. In October of '89, the day after he registered the patent on the Capacitor, he went out to a bar, got flummoxed, and ended up with a telephone pole for a hood ornament."

Sam bit his lip. "Cynthia blamed herself?"

"Must have. I've got a suspicion Roger blamed himself, too. He never wrote another word." After brief consultation with the handlink, he added, "He lived off his royalties and the film sale until '94, when the savings-and-loan mess wiped him out. Right now he's data processing in Kalamazoo." Al shuddered. "Jeez, I'd rather be in—"

"Philadelphia!" Sam supplied, wondering where the reference had popped up from.

For a change, Al was helpful—if sarcastic. "Thank you, W. C. Fields."

Wickedly inclined to follow up on the advantage as he sorted papers, Sam said, "Am I to understand that Kalamazoo is one of the few towns you *don't* have a gal in?"

Al heaved a martyred sigh. "Why is it you always forget everything except just enough to make rotten jokes with?"

Throwing him a smug grin, Sam set aside another pile of magazines and kept searching.

"Ziggy's pretty sure you're here to win Cynthia away from Roger. From what I saw at the joust, she's inclined in Philip's direction anyway. He's just too nerdy to do anything. So all you have to do is romance her until she gets the idea, and—"

"And meantime find Philip's notes for the Capacitor."

Al raised his eyebrows, then frowned deeply. He didn't say anything. He didn't have to.

"I can do both, damn it! This is a chance, Al! I can go through his stuff here, search his office and apartment if I have to—"

"What about Cynthia?"

"I'll just keep things sort of slow," he said, hedging, "and not tell her how he feels until I find what I'm looking for."

"You know it doesn't work that way."

"Stop saying that."

"What if something happens to force the pace? And it will, Sam. It always does."

Sam closed his eyes. After a moment he asked, "If I get them together and they get married, Philip will live, right?"

"Ziggy says that's a one-hundred-percenter."

"What about Roger?"

"What *about* Roger?"

Looking at his partner again, he asked, "Does he write more books? Philip's death and the divorce must've hit him hard."

"Oh—you mean writer's block due to guilt? Hmm. No odds, but I'd say it's likely he'd do more books if nothing happened to Philip."

Sam took a deep, steadying breath. "What about the Capacitor?"

"Well, you gotta admit a honeymoon with Cynthia would be a distraction. . . ." Al stopped. "I don't like what I think you're thinking, Sam."

"You don't have any idea what I'm thinking."

"Oh, no?"

"No."

"Then look me in the eye."

It cost him, but he did it.

"Now," Al ordered, "tell me you're *not* thinking that if Philip doesn't bury himself in his research and lives happily ever after with Cynthia instead, the Capacitor won't be invented for us to use in Project Quantum Leap."

"That's not what I was thinking."

"Sam, when are you gonna learn that you can't lie to me?"

This was getting much too dicey. He needed some kind of distraction, and because his dehydrated innards needed something to drink, Sam slid the ice chest from under the table. Sodas, beers (he opened one immediately and took a swig), cheese, candy bars, a salami—and a huge envelope wrapped in plastic. He stared at it for a blank moment, then set the beer can aside and hefted the package from the ice. About 800 pages of $8\frac{1}{2}$ by 11 paper emerged from plastic and manila and tape.

"What's that?"

"Looks like a report." He riffled the unwieldy mass of pages, too excited to read any of the typescript. "Maybe a treatise on the theory—but there aren't any diagrams."

"Philip didn't leave any notes. That was always the problem. It drove you crazy until I scraped up funding to buy a second one. You took it apart to see how it ticked. And left it in a hundred pieces on the lab bench, Tina says to remind you."

Sam wasn't listening anymore. His gaze had finally focused on a remarkable paragraph. He read it out loud, more amazed with every word.

> *"When first he beheld her beauteous visage, her silken sun-kissed tresses, her rose-petal-lips, her luminescent sapphire orbs, he knew himself gladly, gloriously, and eternally enslaved by the noble and puissant Lady Alix de Courteney, for whom he would slaughter whole armies of perfidious Moors and perish if needs must, her name his dying breath—Alix, Alix—"*

Al's jaw had long since descended toward the tent floor.

"This is *terrible!*" Sam exclaimed. "It's *worse* than terrible!"

The admiral shook himself out of a literary stupor. "It sure as hell ain't quantum physics. Did you say her 'orbs'?"

"It's a manuscript," Sam said in sheer awed disbelief. "A book manuscript. A *lousy* book manuscript!"

"I figured that out, thanks. What I want to know is, what's a 'puissant'?"

"How the hell should *I* know?" He thunked the pages down onto the table, feeling utterly betrayed.

"Knew a girl named Alix once . . . no, twice—" Al abandoned fond reminiscences when Sam glared at him. "One of these days you should check out popular culture. The noble and—whatever—Lady Alix de Courteney just happens to be the heroine of Roger's book. But what's Philip doing with the manuscript

38

of *Knights of the Morningstar?*"

Sam stared down at the first page, emblazoned with title and author.

"I think because Philip *wrote* it."

CHAPTER
FOUR

Once upon a time—it didn't matter which time, because Al remembered it quite clearly and that was the important thing—Thelma Beckett had arrived in New Mexico to visit her younger son. She lived in a condo in Hawaii these days near Katie and her family; the Indiana farm was far behind her. Thelma had sold the land to Beckett kin a few years after her husband's death, so it stayed in the family. But she had never been back.

"I suppose I could've kept on," she'd said to Al over a late-night brandy. "But the house was so big with just Katie and me in it, and it only got bigger once she went away."

Al nodded comprehension of the reference to Katie's ill-considered elopement at age seventeen. No Beckett had spoken the name of the regrettable Chuck since the divorce.

"Of course, I never could have kept the farm as long as I did without Ralph and Suzie and their boys coming to live with us that second summer. It just seemed right to sell it to them."

"Better them than that big corporation Sam told me about," Al agreed.

"Money had best not be everything to a person," Thelma Beckett replied. "I thought I taught Sam that, but his letters are all full of the cost of this and the price of that. He's forever complaining about tightfisted committees back in Washington."

"It's the Project, Mrs. Beckett. Actually, I don't think Sam knows the cost of a quart of milk."

"Well, he wouldn't, growing up on a dairy farm." She smiled. "And I thought I told you to call me by my first name."

He grinned back and gave her a courtly bow— quite an accomplishment, considering he was sitting down. "Formality preserves the proprieties, ma'am."

Her eyes twinkled. "Albert Calavicci! I'm drinking your brandy and sitting in your quarters and it's past midnight—and I'm near old enough to be *your* mother—and you're talking proprieties?"

"Tina's the jealous type. Can I pour you a bit more of this?"

They talked of Hawaii for a time, and how different it was from Indiana, and how different New Mexico was from both. And at length they came to the subject both of them had intended from the first to discuss. Sam.

"Why is he doing this, Albert?" she asked softly. "With all the things he might have chosen to work on, with all his knowledge and his education—why does he want to travel in time?"

"Because nobody's ever done it before." He heard how that sounded, and hastened to add, "Not that Sam's egocentric, wanting to do something that's

41

never been done just so his name and work will be unique. He just—he's curious."

"There's more to it than that," she said vigorously. "I know my son. I birthed him, wiped his nose, and swatted his bottom, and I know how that boy's heart works even if I can't understand where his brain takes him." She paused, a bemused smile touching her lips. "John and I never did work out how plain old farm folk like us produced a certified genius. Sam should've been born to geniuses, or at least somebody rich, who could've given him all the things he should've had—"

"Thelma, that is exactly what he *didn't* need. What you gave him, the way he grew up, that was the best possible thing for him. That's how it was meant to be."

She gave a little shrug. When she spoke again, her voice had softened. "And what about the past, Albert? Isn't *history* the way it was meant to be? Oh, I know why Sam's doing this. He wants to find out what went wrong. But who's to say it *did* go wrong?"

Al gazed into his glass. "Sam thinks some things did," he replied slowly. "I'm not sure I don't agree with him. I mean, you look at the bum deals some people get in life, and it makes you mad. Not just individual people, but whole countries. I think Sam wants to find out why history happened the way it did, so it doesn't happen the same way again. The old saw about those who don't learn from history being condemned to repeat it."

"Condemned," she echoed.

"He wants to know what's behind the What If questions. For instance, what if the Allies had

42

bombed the railroads to the concentration camps? We know fewer Jews would have died. But why didn't it happen that way? Sam can't find that out specifically, of course, because he'll only be able to Leap within his own lifetime."

"Is that the theory?" She smiled again when he frowned slightly in reaction to the skepticism in her voice. "Oh, I don't doubt Sam's equations, Albert. I'm just wondering if he's included all the variables."

Al blinked.

"Have any of you considered what God might think about all this jumping around in Time?" She paused, making a face. "Gracious, just listen to me—calling the Almighty a 'variable'!"

Al considered. Einstein had said that God wasn't a crapshooter, but how did you figure Deity into calculations for quantum physics?

"Umm . . ." He fumbled for a response.

But Thelma Beckett had returned to the original topic with all the directness of mind she had bequeathed to her son. "Sam's interested in great events, then. Things like if the President and Mrs. Kennedy had been in a bulletproof car that day in Dallas. . . ." She sighed, shaking her head. "Do you know what I think? I think Sam's studied so many subatomic particles he's forgotten what they build."

Al glanced up, puzzled. "I'm not sure I know what you mean."

"Of course you don't." She gave him a look of fond exasperation. "You're as bad as he is. Sam knows everything there is to know about all these tiny things nobody ever thinks about. And that's

43

what most people are, Albert—millions of them who *aren't* involved in great events. They live out their lives with only their families to notice, and their names only show up in the county recorder's office under Births, Marriages, and Deaths."

"And Divorces," he added with a wince; Wife Number Five was balking over the settlement again.

"That's another discussion—and don't think I'm leaving here without giving you a good talking-to, Albert Calavicci," she stated.

"Yes, ma'am," he answered meekly. "What about Sam and subatomic particles?"

"Well, what is it they do? As I understand it, they join together and make things."

"The way people join together and make societies?"

"Just like that." She set her empty glass aside and folded her hands in her lap, with an air of having explained the whole matter to her own exacting specifications.

Al struggled to keep up—his usual sensation in Beckett company. "So what you're saying is that it's not the big events that make history. It's the people who form the society where the events happen."

She tilted her head slightly to one side, and Al suddenly saw the girl who—by Sam's telling of it—knocked John Beckett's socks off the first time he clapped eyes on her.

"A rock rolls down a hill when somebody pushes it," she said. "But both the rock and the hill have to be there first."

It was his first intimation—a year before the breakthrough that led to Sam's random Leaps—

that Time didn't focus on the so-called Great. The anonymous, the overlooked, the unremarked and unremarkable: they were the stuff of which history was truly fashioned.

In her plainspoken way, Thelma Beckett had voiced the theory that there were inalterable trends and inevitable tendencies in history. That even if Torquemada had never shown up, someone like him would have; thousands would have burned no matter who sat in the Grand Inquisitor's chair. If Julius Caesar had died at birth, someone like him would have stepped into the power void; though Rome would have lacked his unique military brilliance, it would have kept expanding anyhow.

A variant of the same theory could be applied to individual genius. No matter what went on sociopolitically, Beethoven would have composed, Michelangelo would have sculpted and painted (well, maybe not the latter, considering how he felt about doing the Sistine Chapel), Edison would have invented, and the Beatles would have rocked and rolled. Hell, look at Sam Beckett: even if nobody had ever thought up quantum physics, he still would have made some kind of mark on the world. True genius must serve itself or burn to ashes in its own fire. To use Thelma's metaphor, it always put its shoulder to one rock or another.

The point was that there were thousands of rocks atop millions of hills, and sooner or later *somebody* gave them a push.

It was therefore fairly hopeless to consider changing history—or to change the future based on lessons learned from history—because although trends and tendencies were recognizable, they were simply too large to manage. And while Al had read and loved every single one of Isaac Asimov's *Foundation* novels, he didn't see Sam as Hari Seldon, inventing a version of psychohistory to predict those trends and attempt to steer or at least mitigate them.

So what was the point of Quantum Leaping? Sam was convinced that it was to learn, to find out the whys of the past so that in similar circumstances similar mistakes could be avoided. After his talk with Sam's mother, Al wasn't so sure. And once Sam began his uncontrolled Leaps, he knew Thelma Beckett had been right.

You couldn't change the whole world. But you could change little bits of it for the better, one life at a time. Move a rock so it wouldn't be there to push down that particular hill.

Flattening the hill was harder. But sometimes Sam even managed to do that.

This time, though, Al saw a mountain looming, and the distinct possibility of avalanche.

When Sam was upset, he moved. Indoors, he paced. Outdoors, he ran. It was as if all the negative energy of his anger, confusion, fear, frustration, or any combination of same sluiced down his body to his heels and thence into carpet, earth, or concrete. Grounding the energy, Al thought, giving it somewhere to go before it blew up.

He wavered between two interpretations of Sam's habit. First, that because that off-the-IQ-scale mind was usually faster than his troubles, Sam figured his feet ought to be just as fast. Second, that he was in effect stomping his problems into the ground.

Today Sam held himself to a steady, long-limbed walk through the campground. Al kept an eye on him, centered on him and popping in and out as Sam put distance between himself and the disappointing briefcase and that damn fool manuscript. After a time, when Sam finally slowed down, Al positioned himself directly ahead of him on the footpath leading through the forest.

"Dr. Beeks says it's common among you big-brain types," he began, his delivery deliberately breezy. "You need a recreational outlet, something completely removed from your research. Richard Feynman pounded on bongo drums. Einstein played the fiddle."

"And Philip Larkin wrote trashy novels. *Bad* trashy novels, if that's not a redundancy."

"I don't suppose you remember *your* little hobby."

Sam stopped walking and eyed him warily. "I—I play piano, and guitar . . . and sing a little. . . ."

Gotcha! Al hid a grin. "Does the word 'hula' conjure up any memories?" he asked, Grouchoing his cigar suggestively.

"Al!"

"Tina always said you looked cute in a sarong. But not as cute as *me*," he ended with a self-satisfied swagger.

It worked. Sam laughed, some of the tension draining away. "For a minute there I thought you were going to say 'a grass skirt and a coconut brassiere.'"

"Well, there was that time Gushie and I got you plastered on mai tais. . . ."

"Nice try," Sam scoffed. "I'm allergic to rum."

Mission accomplished. Back to business. "How about mead?"

Sam looked blank.

"You'll be drinking it at the banquet tonight. It's fermented honey," Al explained. "Kick like a moose on the loose. Think of it as the Jack Daniel's of the fifteenth century."

Sam made an angry, dismissive gesture. "I'm not going to the banquet."

So much for easing tension. "You have to. Even if you do have two jobs here, fixing up Philip with Cynthia is the main concern."

"Whose main concern? Theirs, mine, or Ziggy's?" Sam didn't wait for an answer. Long legs in knee-topping leather boots took him quickly up the footpath.

A stab at the handlink flashed Al into the space immediately ahead of Sam again. He was fairly sure his friend wouldn't just plow through him; hologram or not, the evidence of his eyes was not easily ignored. He was right. Sam stopped, and even though the face was Philip Larkin's, the expression on it was pure Beckett mulishness.

"Everybody's," Al said in response to the last question.

Sam kicked at a loose rock, caroming it off a tree root. "It's been so long, Al," he muttered. "Every so often I get a little taste of hope, or home—I know because I remember things. Faces, feelings . . . not exactly what I did, or anything except pieces of what happened, but—" Another rock went sailing. "I just know that home is still there for me, people I love—even if I can't remember their names."

Al had heard some of this before. Loneliness, resentment, longing for home—and who could blame him? More than four years of this. Four years of being other people, living bits of their lives, putting things right for them—while living his own life was denied him.

But there was something different about Sam's depression this time. Something deeper. *Shock treatment*, Al told himself, instantly flinching from the term. The worst it had ever been, the cruelest he had ever had to be, had come after a literal shock treatment in a mental institution. They'd almost lost Sam that time.

"Do it, Sam! Tell them—or you'll never see me again!"

He rejected the memory, then grabbed at it for guidance in how to beat his best friend over the head again—God help him.

"You sound awful damned sorry for yourself," he said harshly.

Sam blinked. "It's not that."

"Sure sounds that way."

"It's not!" he protested. "I'm only trying to understand why it happens. Why I Leap into situations that directly touch my own life. I thought once that it was a reward for a job well done."

"Maybe it is, Sam."

"Yeah, right."

Another stone went flying from the toe of his boot, right through Al's kneecap. Deliberate? Al chose not to consider that.

"So what's your point?" he challenged.

"The point?" Sam impacted a fist against the tree trunk. "The point is I've wised up. I'm slow sometimes, but I'm not stupid. A glimpse of home is the carrot that keeps the poor dumb donkey plugging along."

It was even worse than Al had guessed. Bitterness etched every word in acid. Shock wasn't going to do it; deliberate therapeutic cruelty was out of the question. Al just couldn't, not when Sam looked and sounded this way.

"What's going on here, Al?" Sam went on, angrier by the moment. "Is it *compassion* that puts me in places where I can maybe do myself some good? Or is it just accidental?" His mouth drew into a sneering line Al would have bet the Pentagon's annual budget he'd never see. " 'Oh, by the way, while you're straightening out so-and-so's life, you can see your father again—' "

"You remember those times?" Al asked quietly. "Seeing people you knew before?"

Sam's shoulders jerked up and down, and he started walking again. "I remember a little," he said as Al hurried to catch up. "Enough to keep going. To keep hoping. And that's why it happens. It's just—"

He spun around, both hands lifted as if to grasp something that wasn't there, then falling helplessly to his sides.

"I'm *tired*, Al. Do you have any idea how tired? I want to go home. And I'm beginning to think that Whatever or Whoever is Leaping me around won't *let* me go home. *Ever.*"

(The air nearby shimmered with more than the afternoon heat. A slim, predatory redhead materialized from the middle of a chaotic rainbow. From the pocket of her crimson silk suit—which Al would have recognized as an Yves St. Laurent knockoff and scorned as lacking the *maestro*'s class—she drew a small complex rectangle that chittered and whirred at her.)

"You're just tired, Sam, like you said. It'll work out."

"Will it? When?"

(The redhead glanced around, startled—then pursed her lips in a long, appreciative whistle when she caught sight of Sam Beckett. "Well! If it isn't the studly darling himself! Lothos! Jackpot!")

Al tried again. "Quantum Leaping is your dream, Sam. You're in the middle of it, living it—how many people get to live their dreams?"

"When do I wake up?" Sam countered. "When do I get to climb out of my own bed and see my own face in a mirror? My God, Al, I've almost forgotten what I look like!"

(The woman sauntered closer, taking a visual tour. "Mmmm . . . 1.85 meters, give or take, about 80 kilos arranged with perfect taste—but when did you trim your hair, sweet cheeks?" She circled Sam, moving through a sapling as if it didn't exist, and perused him at lustful leisure. "I must say, you've improved sartorially since last we met— or didn't meet, more's the pity. Alia has all the luck. I approve the poet's shirt. And have I ever mentioned how black leather boots affect my blood pressure?")

"What if I *do* get home?" Sam demanded. "What happens next? Do I send somebody else into the Accelerator? I can't do that. I *won't*. I know what it's like, I know what kinds of temptations come with every Leap—"

"You won't let anybody else do the work because you're the only one you trust to do it right?" Al felt his facial muscles pull into a snarl. "That's pretty damned arrogant, if you ask me."

("Having a little heart-to-heart with your hologram sidekick?" the woman asked Sam. "Pity I can't hear his side of things. But *you* are simply fascinating me. Say on, dear boy, say on.")

"Who says I've done so great? Who says that for every single thing I've put right, something else didn't go wrong?"

("We do our best," she murmured silkily. "Though I suppose you'd call it our worst. It's all a matter of semantics.")

"Even if that were true," Al argued, "don't you trust that if it was bad enough, you'd Leap back in and—"

"I'm fresh out of blind faith, Al. I trust me, and I trust you, and that's about it."

"Should I be flattered?" Al flung his cigar on the Imaging Chamber floor and stomped on it. The instant it left his hand it became invisible to Sam. Al dug his heel into the crushed tobacco viciously. A genuine Havana at ten bucks a smoke, and he was so mad he'd wasted half of it, and it was all Sam's fault. Al wished he could grab him by the shoulders and shake some sense into him.

"Let's say you *are* home," he grated. "You won't *allow* anybody else into the Accelerator. So what're you gonna do? Huh? Go on vacation? A month on the beach at Maui? Go visit Paris again—" He bit back the rest; he'd been about to say *with Donna*, and she would've had his hide for it.

"I don't know!" Sam cried. "But it'd be nice to have the option for a change! How long has it been since I had any choice about where I go or what I do? I'm tired of this!"

("Oh, poor baby!" the woman cooed.)

"So what happens when you get back from your little R and R?" Al pressed. "Do you jump back into the Accelerator and start all over again? Or do you shut the whole Project down?"

Sam backed off, as Al had hoped he would. Confusion and pain were difficult enough to watch in his face, even filtered through someone else's features, but they were preferable to despair.

"I—I don't know," Sam faltered. "I'm not sure what I'd do. But don't you see that that's exactly why I won't be allowed to find out? I'm never getting home, Al. Whatever I do about Philip and Cynthia and Roger and that stupid book, whatever does or doesn't happen, none of it matters. I can do everything I'm supposed to, make everything right—*and it won't matter*. I'm never going home. *Never!*"

This time he ran headlong. Al didn't follow. He watched Sam vanish up the hill into the trees, then muttered, "Ziggy, get me the hell outta here."

(The woman stretched her arms wide, laughing. "Poor darling boy! Homesick, are we? Resenting our role as cosmic fix-it man? And here I thought you

53

were the perfect Hero! There may be hope for you yet." Spinning around on one spike heel, she stabbed at the box in her hand. "Don't you fret, lovey. Aunt Zoey and Cousin Alia will make it *all* better!")

CHAPTER
FIVE

For most of the afternoon, Sam sat on a rock.

He knew he probably ought to be with Cynthia. But solitude was a rare treat—and considering his mood, he wouldn't have been very effective as a lovelorn medievalist, anyway.

So he sat, and thought, and after a while stopped thinking. Clouds slid by above whispering trees, summer wind brought dry scents of sage and pine, sunlight baked soothing warmth into his aching muscles, and for once his mind let him be. Just *be*, without worrying or striving, without planning or calculating or wondering. It was almost—almost— serenity.

Eventually he returned down the hill to the campground. After the joust, the run, and the dusty hill, by now he didn't need just a shower; he needed a car wash.

Philip Larkin's duffel bag yielded a white terry cloth robe and yellow rubber thongs. Armed with these and the shaving kit of toiletries, Sam joined the line leading to ten green plastic cubicles that bore a striking resemblance to portable potties.

His dream was doomed: there was no hot water left. This would not have been a problem earlier in the day, but the July heat had faded by the time Sam got his turn in one of the boxes; when he emerged the sun was gone and the breeze still blowing. He shivered his way back to the tent, telling himself cold was good therapy for sore muscles.

The duffel bag also contained Philip's "mundane" clothes (including, inevitably, a pocket protector) for driving back to New York City, plus a madly romantic costume for this evening's banquet. Wincing, Sam dutifully donned the white linen shirt, sleeveless tunic of tapestry cloth in various burgundies and greens, and black leather belt with sheathed dagger. He drew the line at the hose and velvet slippers, both in a shade of bright yellow Al would have called "lemon" and Sam would have called "lurid." The tan trousers and black boots of this afternoon would have to do. He ran a comb one last time through his damp hair, and snuffed the Coleman lantern.

Thus girded for another battle with Roger/Rannulf, he followed the crowd to the picnic area.

A picnic area it might be in the twentieth century, but a benevolent wizard had transformed it into an open-air medieval banquet hall that sat nearly two hundred. Sam paused beneath a tree, a smile breaking slowly over his face, and for the first time he got a feel for what the Medieval Chivalry League found so enchanting.

The "hall" was formed of elderly oaks and chestnuts, arching a leafy canopy above thirty picnic tables arranged in a horseshoe. Strung from branches and swagged between trees were strings of pinpoint Christmas tree lights. The tables, draped with royal purple cloths, glowed with glass-shielded candles nestled amid braided flowers and vines. Mugs and goblets and tankards shone silvery bright, winking with gems. Never mind, Sam thought with a smile, that the jewels were paste, or that the plates were paper and the knives and spoons plastic. These people—these dreamers—with their low-cut gowns, flashing necklaces, and velvet doublets, with their courtly manners and their belief in honor and handcrafts and plain old rollicking fun—they were in their way as much time travelers as Sam himself.

They were certainly enjoying it more. And their enthusiasm was catching. Sam—Sir Percival—was directed by a page to a seat just below the High Table, where the king and queen sat with their nobility. He was not quite exalted enough to join them, but neither was he placed below the salt. This they took very literally; people seated at the lower end of the horseshoe regularly sent someone up to beg a few pinches of salt from the privileged.

At irregular intervals the herald called out a name or names, and performers would step into the hollow of the horseshoe. Jugglers, mimes, dancers, troubadours playing anything from lutes to finger cymbals, and one Declaimer of Epic Poesy (who bore an astonishing resemblance to Sam's idea of Falstaff) entertained the diners. Sam gathered from the tokens handed out by various nobles that the performances earned points as well as applause.

As Sam dug into slices of succulent beef and roasted potatoes, he began to relax and enjoy himself. He chatted with the dignified middle-aged knight on his left and the younger lady on his right—when she wasn't admonishing her adolescent son to eat his vegetables.

He was halfway through the meal when a pair of ladies sat down opposite him, plates laden and goblets full. The tall, brown-eyed, bespectacled lass was formidably gowned in scarlet and gold, with a pointed headdress trailing five feet of chiffon. Her companion, less flamboyantly clad but all the more exotic for being a Korean damsel in medieval French dress, settled her pearl-gray skirts and turned a stubborn frown on her friend.

"Mel Gibson, and that's final!"

"Yeah, right—they can call it *Mad Max and the Merry Men*. They'll go with a real Brit, maybe Gabriel Byrne—"

"Sally"—with infinite patience—"he's Irish."

"Whatever, he's gorgeous." Sally pulled her dagger from its belt sheath and started slicing potatoes. "All I know is that a friend of mine who got a job with Industrial Light and Magic is going out with a woman whose cousin works for the studio that's developing a script. It won't even start filming until '90 or so. Don't worry, Jen, there's plenty of time to argue about who'll get the lead."

"Mel Gibson," Jen insisted.

"Gabriel Byrne. Or maybe Michael Praed, or—"

"*Mel Gibson!*"

"Umm . . . Kevin Costner, actually," Sam said.

"*What?*" exclaimed both ladies.

"The Robin Hood movie. I've just got this feeling that—"

"Kevin Costner?" Jen asked, wide-eyed. "Kevin 'Perfect Tush' Costner?"

"What have you heard?" Sally demanded. "Do you know somebody? Who's going to play Maid Marian? And what about the Sheriff?"

"It's just a guess," he offered apologetically.

"Kevin Costner," mused Jen. "I like it."

"But he's from *California*!" Sally wailed.

"So's my mother. So what?"

"But—it'd be like casting Michael J. Fox to play the Vampire Lestat!"

After due consideration, Sam thought it the better part of wisdom not to mention who *would* play Lestat.

A blond serving wench—aproned, barefoot, and lugging two huge pitchers of wine—paused on her way past. "Hey, Phil—I mean, Sir Percy—I found an article on that quantum physics guy from M.I.T. You know, the one with the crazy theory about time travel? I'll drop it by your tent before I leave tomorrow."

Mouth full of heady mead, Sam managed to nod. In July of 1987 he'd been not quite thirty-four years old—a bit early for an article in a national magazine. Probably one of those boy-genius, whiz-kid, All-American-farmgrown-Einstein stories that had been popular before the Nobel. And after the Nobel. The media would have devoured him for lunch with hollandaise sauce and a cask of White Zinfandel if he hadn't fled to New Mexico.

There might be a certain morbid fascination in reading the article. But even if he learned things he didn't remember about himself circa 1987, what good would it do him? He'd only forget it all in the next Leap.

Just as he was refusing to get depressed again, a mandolin-toting minstrel approached the High Table. An extravagant bow and the doffing of his cap produced a groan from Sally.

"Oh, God! Not 'Greensleeves' again!"

"He wouldn't dare," glowered the middle-aged knight on Sam's left. "Not even Larry would dare."

"Break out the earplugs," Sally said resignedly.

"Relax," Jen replied. "Our gracious Queen Elinor will tell him to sing 'Sumer Is Icumen In,' at which point King Steffan the Tone-deaf will holler 'cuckold' instead of 'cuckoo,' and Larry will be in disgrace. Again."

Sally giggled all over her round, bespectacled face. "Is he still sleeping with Charlene?"

"He thinks he can make Cynthia jealous. As if she even looks at anybody except—"

"Shh!"

Sam, remembering at the same time as the two ladies that he was supposed to be the object of Cynthia's interest, kept his eyes on his plate.

Speaking of Cynthia, where *was* she? In this Grand Tetons of tall pointed headdresses it was impossible to identify her. More to the point—no pun intended—a quick look around convinced him Roger was absent. Extracting himself from the picnic table, he muttered an excuse no one paid attention to and left the banquet.

Roger, gorgeously arrayed in orange velvet and a large Celtic cross pendant, flicked a finger against a stained-glass chime. A moment later Cynthia opened the tent flap and smiled.

"Good even, my lord! Isn't it lovely out tonight?"

He stared. She looked exquisite in blue embroidered with white roses. Instead of a wimple, she wore her blond hair loose to her shoulders, with a silver mesh cap that dripped crystal beads down her forehead and cheeks.

"So this is the Great Medieval Novel."

Startled out of fantasy (and thinking disloyally that she was perfect until she opened her mouth), he looked down at the fat manila envelope under his arm. "Uh—yeah, I guess."

"Well, let's have it."

Helpless, he handed it over. She hefted it experimentally.

"Good God, it must weigh fifteen pounds!"

"Is that bad?" he asked, apprehensive. "Will you have to cut it much?"

She made a face at him. "Can't bear to see a single word of your deathless prose amputated? You first-time authors are all alike."

He had the grace to blush. "Are you sure you want to look at this? It's pretty rough, even for a rough draft."

"That, my good Lord Rannulf, is why God made hardworking underpaid brilliant editors." She unsealed the envelope. "Where's Philip? He disappeared right after the joust."

Roger shrugged. "Probably sulking in his tent. I got past his guard this morning and he hates that." When she looked skeptical, he added impatiently, "He'll get over it. I've known him for years. He's

61

always like this when he loses a joust."

"If you say so."

But she still doubted, and he had to clench his teeth to keep from yelling, *Forget Philip! What about the book?* Exercising a stern self-command his book's hero might have envied, he asked, "Can you tell right away if it's publishable?"

"I can tell if it's something I can hammer into something publishable." She grinned. "The pen isn't just mightier than the sword, Roger—in the hands of an editor, it's infinitely more ruthless."

A nervous laugh escaped him. "Is that a threat or a warning?"

Cynthia winked and started back into the tent.

"You're going to read it now? I mean, the banquet's started, and I thought we'd sit together and everything. . . ."

"I just want a fast look. The light's better inside. Then we'll have something to talk about over the suet pudding."

"Oh God," he moaned. "Tim and Hannah are Wardens of the Royal Cupboard again, aren't they? Who ever told that woman she could cook?"

"Tim, of course. He doesn't have a choice—he's married to her! Well? Aren't you going to come in?"

At any other time he would have accepted instantly. "I think I'll wait out here."

Cynthia shook her head mockingly. Light from the lantern struck soft rainbows from crystal beads. "Scourge of the tourney field, and can't bear to watch a lady read a book! Why don't you go find Philip? I don't like it when you two squabble." She disappeared into the blue tent.

Philip again, Roger thought with a sigh—but she was going to read part of the book. Roger's fate was now in her hands, quite literally—or literarily, to be precise. What would his hero, the Comte de St. Junien, do while he waited on Lady Alix's decision? Not that he'd ever let her decide much of anything, for he was a powerful nobleman and she only the beautiful but impoverished daughter of a minor chevalier. . . .

Roger called St. Junien to mind, writing the scene in his head, and imitated the picture. He lounged against a tree, trying for insouciant grace. Privately he suspected he achieved only ludicrous lurking. But nobody was around to judge one way or the other.

Sam made his way to Cynthia's tent—muttering, gesturing, shaking his head. The few people he encountered showed no sign that this was unusual behavior for Philip Larkin. Not that Sam would have noticed.

"Cynthia, I'm sure you don't know, but—"

He grimaced. "No, she's not dumb. Besides, the way she looked at him this morning—" With a sigh, he tried again.

"Cynthia, I haven't said anything because—Okay, because why? Don't get into the reasons. Be Sir Percival. Gallant, chivalrous, brave, dashing—" One hand over his heart as if about to recite the Pledge of Allegiance, he declared, "Cynthia, my sweet! I love you!"

"Needs some work, Sam," Al said behind him. "You could always use the line about her orbs."

63

Sam gave a violent start. Sometimes Al gave him fair audio warning by opening the Imaging Chamber door nearby. Other times he took unfair technological advantage and popped in elsewhere, then had Ziggy center him on wherever Sam was.

"How many times have I told you—"

"Don't do that," Al finished for him. "Nice threads. But you should be wearing tights with that outfit, Sam."

"No way." Habit made him glance around for potential eavesdroppers. Seeing none, he went on. "I read more of the book, Al—what I could stomach, anyway. Alix de Courteney is obviously supposed to be Cynthia. Blue eyes, blond hair—she even makes wind chimes out of glass left over from building the local cathedral while her lover's away at the Crusades."

"So? Cynthia does look pretty cute in a wimple. She's a natural to model a character after."

"Guess who the lover is."

Al considered. "You mean—nah, not Philip! The Comte de St. Junien is a great big guy, all brawn and bluster—" He broke off. "Oh. Wish fulfillment."

Sam nodded. "You know what *I* wish? That just once I could Leap in *after* the guy has confessed his undying devotion. Why can't anybody say it? Three simple words, one syllable each. How tough can it be?"

Al walked along beside him, waxing philosophical. "It's not saying 'I love you' that's hard, it's meaning it. If I'd understood that years ago, I'd be saving myself three—no, four—sets of alimony checks."

After a moment's hesitation, Sam ventured, "Can

I ask you something about that?"

"Anything except the dollar amount. It's bad for my blood pressure to remember it more than once a month."

"Not about the alimony. About the wives. Why did you marry them all?" He cast a sidelong glance at his partner. "It's not as if you *had* to."

"Because I'm the last of the great romantics. Go ahead, laugh," he invited with a resigned wave of his cigar. "But it's true. I *love* weddings. The music, the flowers, the lacy gown, the champagne—"

"The wedding night?" Sam suggested, grinning.

"That, too." Dark eyes danced with mischief and memories.

"You love weddings, but you're not so hot on marriage, is that it?"

"Basically."

Sam thought about pointing out that he could indulge his penchant for nuptials any Saturday of the year by crashing the local churches. Then he thought better of it. Al, the last of the hopeful romantics, would believe every single time his next ex-wife walked down the aisle that this time the romance would last.

It seemed to Sam that a disproportionate number of Leaps—what he could remember of them, anyway—involved romance, the present one included. Why did people have so much trouble with love? Philip, for instance, could only approach Cynthia through a badly written substitute. Which reminded him of something.

"Al?"

"Yep?"

"The book really is awful. How could anybody publish something that bad?"

Al shrugged. "I guess Cynthia's a much better editor than Philip is a writer. Hell, half the novels I read, I wonder why the publisher paid good money for 'em."

For a few steps they were quiet. After a few more steps, Sam developed a rueful expression. "What I said earlier . . . about home . . ."

Al made it easy on him. "Nobody could blame you for feeling that way, kid. Just don't go overboard the other way and get all guilty. It happened. It's over. Forget it. Want to try out your Cynthia-my-sweet number again? Oops, too late. There's Roger."

Sam spied Philip's rival propping up a tree with one massive shoulder. Setting his jaw, prepared to win Philip's lady fair, Sam started forward. Just then Cynthia emerged from the tent, and Roger straightened up as if he'd swallowed a sword. Sam slid into a shadow.

"Stunned," Cynthia announced. "I'm stunned."

"Oh God." Roger panicked. "I knew it. It's bad— it's worse than bad. It's terrible. You hate it."

Cynthia eyed him judiciously. "Well, it *is* rough. It needs a lot of work. I'm not entirely happy with the opening of Chapter Three, and the motivation is weak when St. Junien tells the king to go take a hike."

"Al!" Sam hissed. "He showed her the book!"

"No foolin', Sherlock."

"But how did he get a copy?"

"How do I know? Shut up and listen."

"On the whole," Cynthia continued, "in my professional opinion . . ." All at once she grinned up at him, then laughed. "Rog, it's potential dynamite!"

"You mean—" The mighty Lord Rannulf went wobbly at the knees. "You're k-kidding."

"I *never* kid about finding a good story," she responded severely. "I slogged the slush pile for two solid years before I found a single halfway readable manuscript. Do you know how much manure I still have to shovel to find one mangy old pony? This is a Thoroughbred in the making—and we've got a chance at the Triple Crown!"

"You—you'll publish my book?"

"After I edit the junk out of it, you'd better believe we'll publish it. But it needs another title. *Knights of Honor* won't sell five copies, even with the hottest cover we can get." She paused. "Remind me to find out if this Fabio guy is available to model for the Comte. He's hot and getting hotter. Anyway, we need a better title. Because if you're taking this relationship between the Comte and Lady Alix where I think you're taking it—"

Roger had recovered from shock and was taking this opportunity to move in. "Something sexy," he said as he leaned closer.

Al strolled over to observe technique.

"But subtle," Cynthia agreed.

"Evocative," murmured Roger.

"But elegant," Cynthia purred, fluttering her lashes as skillfully as Scarlett O'Harra.

Al peered at her in the evening gloom. "Honey, are you really falling for this?"

Roger was no Rhett Butler. "Stolen nights in a castle tower . . ."

"Moonlight shining on the moat . . ."

"I may throw up," Al announced.

Lips mere inches from Cynthia's, Roger whispered, "A minstrel singing love lyrics from a balcony . . ."

They kissed. Cynthia's eyes widened as if she hadn't expected quite this degree of competence—and hadn't expected to enjoy it quite so much. She stepped back and with a slightly forced little laugh said, "And the stench rising from the middens. Get real, Rog. I need a title, not a cliché."

Roger deflated like a popped balloon. Al cheered. Sam grinned to himself; she might look the dainty damsel, but Cynthia Mulloy was twentieth century down to her editor's blue pencil. He almost felt sorry for Roger.

"Well?" Al snapped. "Get in there and start swinging, Sir Percy! Think honor! Think chivalry! Think book royalties!"

"Think about getting out of my way," Sam suggested.

Al sniffed and punched the handlink. A rectangle of light opened, and a moment later he was gone.

Stepping from the shadows, Sam said, "How about *Knights of the Morningstar*? You stole the rest of my book, Roger, why not take my title as well?"

Cynthia gave a little gasp of surprise, and maybe guilt. "Philip? What—?"

"Go on, Roger. Tell her who really wrote what she just read."

Roger drew himself up to his full six feet four inches. "*I* did. And you know damned well I did, Phil!"

Sam advanced menacingly—a piece of purest lunacy, considering his and Roger's relative sizes. "Tell her the truth."

"It *is* the truth!" Roger stood his ground.

Cynthia was the one who backed up a pace, genuinely worried by what she saw in both men's eyes. "Wait a minute. I don't understand. Who wrote the book?"

"I did," they answered simultaneously, exchanged dirty looks, and tried to outtalk each other.

"Alix de Courteney was just the name I used—I didn't know any other way of letting you know how I feel about—"

"I was hoping you'd read the description and recognize yourself as Alix, and find out how I feel about—"

She stuck two fingers in her mouth and gave a piercing, unladylike whistle. "Hold it right there! Shut up!"

They followed this excellent advice, glowering at each other.

"*I'm* Alix? You put *me* into the book?"

"Yes," they chorused.

Cynthia winced. "We'll let that pass for the moment. Roger. You said you hadn't shown it to anyone else."

"I didn't."

"Then how does Philip know the heroine's name?"

Nary a pause for quick thinking. "He must've stolen it from my tent and read it on the sly. He knew I was writing it—"

Sam broke in. "He stole it from *my* tent. If we go there now, it'll be gone. Because it's not there, it's here." This made precious little sense—even to

69

him—so he started over. "Look, I know it sounds lame, but you have to believe me, Cynthia. Would I make up something like this?"

"It sounds incredibly lame," she declared. "I don't know who to believe. What I do know is that in my tent is a novel I can make into a surefire blockbuster. The question is, who wrote the damned thing?"

Turning slightly so Roger couldn't see her face, she placed an unobtrusive hand on Sam's arm. He read her eyes instantly: it was much the same look she'd given him earlier, before the joust. She wanted some sort of sign from him, some kind of proof.

Sam was as tongue-tied now as he'd been this morning. He parted dry lips, hoping something would occur to him.

Something occurred to Cynthia instead. Quickly, eerily, distorted by tiny warping pulses of light, she changed.

And became Alia.

CHAPTER
SIX

Alia!

But Alia it was. Cynthia's touch had been light and pleading; Alia's fingers dug into the muscles of Sam's arm. Cynthia's silver-and-crystal cap had crowned a mane of golden hair; now it rested atop Alia's wheaten chin-length bob. Sapphire eyes had paled, the cheekbones arched higher, and the rose-strewn gown slid down a figure taller and slimmer.

Sam stared down at her in mindless shock.

She smiled, full lips curving with artless innocence, eyes glistening with artful malice. Her whisper was sweet and taunting, pitched to Sam's hearing alone.

"Well, Sam Beckett. You're a difficult man to find."

She removed her hand from his arm and turned, no longer smiling as she let Roger see her face. He, of course, still saw Cynthia.

"The manuscript in your tent is mine," he was saying defiantly. "Philip didn't write a single sentence of it."

Alia turned an earnest gaze on Sam, lips twitching slightly at the corners in silent mockery of his stunned paralysis. "What am I going to do?"

He heard so many meanings in that question that his throat closed even tighter.

"Either I wrote it or Phil wrote it," Roger stated. "It all depends on who you believe, doesn't it, Cynthia?"

"Yes," she said, with a thoughtful nod and a sidelong glance for Sam. "It certainly does."

A horn sounded—that damned herald again, Sam thought, startled out of near catatonia. Alia looked from him to Roger and back again, a frown flickering above bright eyes. All at once she assumed a wild, almost fey look, and Sam knew he had to do something, say something—

"Roger—" he managed, thick-voiced and without the slightest idea of what could follow next.

"What?" Roger growled.

Sam opened his mouth, closed it again. What, indeed? *This isn't Cynthia! She may look like her, but she isn't. Her name is Alia and she's a time traveler from I don't know where or when, and she's here to ruin your life, or Philip's, or Cynthia's, or all three—and mine, too, because I'm not really Philip Larkin—in fact, she may be here to kill me—*

Hopeless.

"*What?*" Roger asked again, and took a threatening step forward. "This isn't the tourney field, Phil, but it's still just you and me. Let's do it. Right here, right now."

"Don't be ridiculous!" Alia suddenly gathered voluminous blue skirts in both hands, heading for the

72

sound of the hunting horn. "Come with me, both of you!"

They followed. Sam figured his bewilderment and Roger's were probably just about equal. He was positive their levels of dread were not. Sam worried most about her confidence—and secretly envied it. The first part of a Leap was, for him, always an exercise in urgent confusion. But Alia seemed to know exactly who everyone was, exactly what was going on, and exactly what she intended to do about it.

She led them down the center of the horseshoe, right past a tangle of acrobats, straight to the High Table. She dipped a low curtsy as King Steffan, crown slightly askew, raised his goblet and smiled welcome.

"Lady Cyndaria! Escorted by *two* noble knights, no less! How fare you this evening, Lord Rannulf, Sir Percival?"

Before Roger could do more than bow—Sam was incapable even of that—Alia spoke up.

"Your Majesties," she said, including the queen, "pray forgive this untimely interruption, but I am convinced that this is a matter you alone can decide."

The king gestured to the herald, whose stentorian yell quieted the crowd at once. The acrobats dropped their act—but, happily, not each other— and withdrew.

"What matter is this, my lady?" asked the king.

"Lord Rannulf and Sir Percival both claim ownership of the same item. Because there is no proof either way of the truth, I beg your wisdom in resolving the problem."

"What the hell is she doing?" Sam hissed at Roger.

"Playing by League rules," was the reply, rich with delight. Roger was settling into his Lord Rannulf role with every evidence of relish. He was actually enjoying this. Anticipating it, even. He didn't know what Sam knew. He had no reason to fear what Sam feared.

"Lady Cyndaria," said Queen Elinor as she dipped her fingers up to the rings in a bowl of water and floating rose petals, then plied a linen square to dry her hands. "You wish us to settle this matter of honor?"

Alia humbly bent her shining head, hiding what Sam knew instinctively was a smug little smile. The crystals brushed her cheeks and forehead with soft color. "If Your Majesty would be so gracious, please."

The queen folded the linen daintily. "There is precedent in resolving such questions, as you know. Lord Rannulf and Sir Percival are aware of it also, I believe."

"Precedent?" Sam asked blankly.

"Ample," the herald put in. "Four years ago, the question of the kingship itself was decided between—"

"We were all there, Harvey," the king interrupted.

"Owain," corrected the queen.

"Whatever," said the king. "Well, my lord? Sir Percival?"

Alia subtly eased herself to one side with the air of a task excellently accomplished. But nothing had happened. Sam was more confused than ever.

Roger thundered his challenge for the benefit of the crowd. "I demand that Sir Percival make public apology for his slanders!"

The crowd loved it. King Steffan held up a hand for quiet. "Silence! We will hear Sir Percival's answer!"

Sam's head spun. Matter of honor—League rules—public apology—be damned! He knew who'd written *Knights of* whatever-it-was, however badly. Philip had lost publication credit and Cynthia and eventually his life because he hadn't had the gumption to stick up for himself. Well, Sam was wearing Philip's Sir Percival persona now, and Sir Percival was about to do the Proper Medieval Thing.

Whatever it was.

Better make a start. "I do not apologize! There is nothing to apologize for!"

"You lie, knave!" Roger roared.

His Majesty looked enthralled.

Her Majesty was not amused. "This conflict distresses us, my lord, Sir Knight. Surely there can be a peaceful solution."

Roger sneered at Sam. "Only if he makes formal amends, Your Majesty. Otherwise—"

A rectangle of white light only Sam could see appeared to Roger's right, and a silhouetted figure stepped through. An instant later the light vanished. Al was clearly visible now, frantically punching the handlink. "Got him, Gushie! Sam! Boy, am I glad I found you! I don't know what's going on, but we lost you for a couple minutes. Ziggy's about to bust a circuit. I've only seen her this way once before—"

He caught sight of Alia.

75

"And that was when! Moses on a pony, Sam, where the hell did *she* come from? What's she doing here? How'd she find you?"

Possessing not the vaguest answer to any of these queries, Sam cast him an anguished look of appeal.

"Otherwise . . ." Roger repeated direly.

"Come, now," said the queen. "There ought to be some way of settling this, short of violence."

"The Rules of Order for disputes between knights—" the herald began, but was glared to silence by His Majesty's piercing green eyes.

"Challenge him," Al urged.

"*What?*"

Sam's request for clarification was interpreted by Roger as an invitation to detail his intentions. He did so with a wide grin.

"To a duel!" Al said. "Trial by combat! Challenge him!"

"Are you crazy?" Sam demanded—of them both.

Roger's grin became a snarl. "Coward!"

King Steffan was frowning. "I like not your tone, Lord Rannulf. Nor your implication, Sir Percival. Her Majesty is right. But while it is ever our hope that we can avoid contention between our noble knights, if this truly is the only way to resolve the difficulty—"

For once, Sam had the luxury of combining two conversations into one—and his reaction to each was total incredulity. "You mean I'm supposed to slap his face with a gauntlet and toss it on the ground at his feet?"

"Sir Percival," asked the queen, "is that your wish?"

Al waved one arm madly, as if signaling Sam on past third to home plate. "Go for it, Percy!"

"I'm not *wearing* a gauntlet, damn it!"

"Sir Knight!" Owain, the herald, exclaimed. "The queen and her ladies are present!"

"Uh—sorry." Sam added a slight bow for good measure. Her Majesty nodded frosty forgiveness. He faced Roger—and beyond him saw Alia, breathless with excitement. Clearing his throat, Sam shouted, "I do not apologize! And I challenge Lord Rannulf to a duel!"

The crowd went wild, and nothing the herald could do would quiet them.

The foot of the royal goblet hit the banquet table with a thunk. "You wish to prove the truth of your claim upon your body?"

"Uh—forsooth." Sam was proud of himself for that one; he felt he was finally getting the hang of this. Warming to his theme, he went on. "Your Gracious Majesties, I hereby demand satisfaction of Lord Rannulf for his lies and slanders and—and calumnies! He stole what belongs to me, and says it is his own!"

"Atta boy, Percy baby!" Al crowed.

The king exchanged whispers with the queen, then addressed Sam once more. "We must needs give fair warning, Sir Percival. Should you be defeated on the field of honor, then his words are proved true." Leaning forward, he continued more softly, "Look, Phil—you sure about this?"

"Your Majesty, I am in the right—as Lord Rannulf well knows!"

Roger looked murderous. "I accept the challenge!

77

And for my own part, I issue a counter-challenge—
for the right to woo and win the fair Lady Cyndaria
of the Chimes!"

Pandemonium.

Trial by combat, questions of honor, chivalrous
contention for the hand of a lady—this was better
than Errol Flynn, the Round Table, and Sir Walter
Scott all rolled into one.

Queen Elinor beckoned Alia forward. "My lady?
Do you agree to the terms of this challenge?"

Wide-eyed and demure, Alia trod lightly to the
High Table, smiling like a cat with dollops of cream
still on her whiskers. "I am unworthy of causing
such dissension, Your Majesty. But far be it from
me to interfere in matters of chivalry between noble
knights."

The king thumped a fist on the table, rattling the
platters. "Well-spoken, Lady Cyndaria!"

Resigned to the inevitable, the kindhearted queen
sighed. "My liege, will you name the hour?"

"Herald, clear a place in tomorrow's lists." King
Steffan raised his voice to address the throng. "Be
it known by all here present that Sir Percival has
issued challenge to Lord Rannulf on a matter of
honor, and that Lord Rannulf has issued counter-
challenge for the favor of the fair Lady Cyndaria.
Until tomorrow on the field of combat!"

Cheers abounded, cups were lifted high, and
wagers flew thick and fast. Sam, in that moment,
honestly hated Alia for what she'd done—not to him
or even to Roger or Cynthia, but to these people
all around him. What had been a sweet, harmless,
elaborate conspiracy among romantic dreamers, Alia

had turned into something darker. It was up to him to keep them happily ignorant of the possibly deadly truths behind this innocent medieval charade.

Watching her face as she accepted a seat at the High Table and a cup of wine, he amended "possibly" to "probably."

CHAPTER SEVEN

> *. . . finished his prayer and made the sign of the cross just before he Leaped.*
> *Here endeth the Priest's Tale.*

Donna Alisi Beckett hit the SAVE key on her office terminal and smiled. If Al was Sancho to Sam's Don Quixote, she had taken on the role of Dr. Watson to her husband's Sherlock Holmes, rendering each Leap in prose. Ziggy regarded this story-telling as scornfully as Holmes viewed Watson's efforts until Donna suggested a perusal of the only tale the Great Detective himself had written. The Master had confessed himself, if not humbled, then at least mildly chastened by the difficulty of the literary task. Ziggy had reacted with a thoughtful silence. Ever since, she looked forward to Donna's stories—and complained if she didn't get enough lines.

At first Donna had tried to keep up with the Leaps in chronological order—not by the years Sam was in but by the sequence here in her own time. Some stories, though, she found she was incapable of writing down. Not necessarily the ones when Sam got involved with another woman—she had recorded the three Leaps centered around Abigail Fuller, Sammy Jo's mother—but the ones that had hurt emotionally.

She knew, for example, that she would never be able to write about the agonizing Leap into the mental institution. She could still see in memory the reddened wounds on his temples when he'd come back to her for those twelve brief hours. And she had not yet found resilience enough to record the Leap in which she herself had been a prominent player. There were others; she tried not to think about them too much.

But some she wrote about for the sheer joy of remembering the people involved, especially those she had come to know in the Waiting Room. Jimmy, with his eager, sunny smile. Sam himself as a teenager, with his blush and stammer—which evened the score, because now *she'd* met *him* as a kid, too. The young Al, who had ogled her legs to the infuriated mortification of his elder self. Samantha Stormer—bright, ambitious, determined to succeed in the chauvinistic sixties. And of course Jesse, the elderly black man whose reaction to seeing a young white man in the mirrored table had been a polite request that they give him his own face back. "Ain't the prettiest face in the wide sweet world, but I lived with it nigh on sixty years, near's I can figger. I'm used to it by now, Missie."

Donna included the New Mexico end of each Leap in every story, because when Sam came home he would want to know. She wrote for him, and because of him. Telling each tale made her feel closer to him. If she could not share his life as it happened, the way Al did, she could at least participate after the fact, and crystallize her own understanding.

Verbeena Beeks had no luxury of choice. Sometimes they didn't see her for days as she frantically recorded the last Leap's data before the current one caught up with her. Ziggy helped, of course, keeping track of everything for congressional funding's sweet sake. Not that Ziggy ever told everything she knew to governmental computers; she found them slow, stupid, and silly, not worthy of the energy it took to interface—energy she usually charged to their electric bills, not hers. For Ziggy, it was the equivalent of going out to a bad dinner and sticking her blind date with the check.

"Well?" Donna said to thin air. "How do you like it?"

"Interesting and entertaining, Dr. Alisi. One might even say morally uplifting. But I don't understand the last sentence."

She sipped at a cup of lukewarm Earl Grey tea. "A little joke, Ziggy. Cross-reference Chaucer."

There was barely a pause. "Oh. I see. A tip of the metaphorical hat to a literary tradition. Do you plan to publish?"

"Lord, no!" She laughed. "Who'd believe it?"

"Dr. Alisi, this is *not* science fiction."

"Not to us, maybe."

Ziggy ruminated. Then: "The financial rewards might be substantial."

Donna shut down the terminal and stretched the stiffness from her shoulders. Neanderthal neck: the curse of all writers. "Worried about your credit rating again?"

"The last subcommittee meeting went very well, Dr. Alisi. I anticipate no difficulties. I am merely impressed by Roger Franks's royalties."

She laughed again. "Good night, Ziggy."

"Good night, Dr. Alisi. Pleasant dreams."

"Same to you."

Donna closed the door behind her and walked down the hall to the mess. She had more to do tonight, and there was a rumor that Sam's mother had express-mailed coconut macaroons. Cookie jar raided and teacup replenished, Donna continued through the maze of corridors to her sleeping quarters.

She paused with her fingers hovering beside the light switch, wondering if anything had changed within. Al said that sometimes when he visited Sam's office, things were different. A photograph in a different place on a wall; a scribble on a notepad that hadn't been there before; the desk clock on the left instead of the right. He found it occasionally unnerving, and every so often a little scary.

Because Al lived each Leap with Sam, he had two sets of memories: before and after. As each Leap developed, Ziggy shunted "before" data to one bank as a control. Al had to do pretty much the same thing—but the human brain was not as tidy a computer. Mostly it was easy, for the lives Sam changed were remote from his own. But sometimes he suffered from severe psychological indigestion. Verbeena decided that it was only Al's land-on-your-feet-not-on-your-face adaptability that kept him sane. Ziggy might *know* two histories, but Al *experienced* them.

The rest of the team had only Ziggy's and Al's word for it that things had changed at all. Insofar as Donna knew, for example, Jacqueline Kennedy Onassis had lived in New York City for at least twenty-five years. But Ziggy said, and Al confirmed, that she had survived that terrible day in Dallas because of Sam. The rest of the team had perforce learned to shrug off frustration when told their memories had changed with the changes Sam made. That history always altered for the better made it easier, of course.

The only real evidence Donna or Gushie or Tina or Verbeena had that time had rearranged its shape was the little frown on Al's face whenever he noticed something different. Once, when he and Donna were in Albuquerque for dinner—a rare break from the Project mess hall—he'd complimented her on her "new" turquoise earrings. They'd been a Christmas present from Sam seven years ago, and she wore them four days out of ten, but Al behaved as if he'd never seen them before. Donna spent the rest of the evening wondering what minor sideslip in time had caused Sam to buy these earrings instead of the scarf or bracelet that had been her Christmas present in another timeline.

Small things, these changes. She never noticed them. As far as she was concerned, there were never any changes to be noticed. But every so often she paused in the doorway of her office or bedroom, wondering what might have appeared or vanished or switched position while she was gone.

Not that she would ever know. But for some reason, it bothered her.

In the end, she left the main lights off. No need for them, anyway. Crossing to the bed, she flicked on the bedside reading light and turned back the sheets. After dressing in a pair of Sam's pajamas, she settled down with pillows to prop her back and spent a few minutes with eyes closed thinking about exactly nothing.

Then, rousing herself from the short meditation, she adjusted the lamp and took a flat plastic case from the table. She had long since learned to use her personal laptop for personal correspondence. Ziggy was a snoop.

Sitting cross-legged with tea and cookies in reach, she began typing a letter to her sister-in-law.

Dear Katie,

Many thanks for the birthday goodies. They arrived two days ago and if you think those gorgeous papayas went uneaten until my birthday today, think again! Thank Lizzie for her beautiful watercolor, which is now on my office wall. By the way, am I to assume that the ASTRONO-MERS DO IT STARRY-EYED T-shirt means that a certain nephew will be following in his mother's footsteps?

Your question wasn't nosy at all. I'm glad you asked, in fact, because it gives me the chance to talk about it—on paper, anyhow.

By way of an answer—most of the time I'm all right, but sometimes not so all right. I think rather often about what Al's first wife Beth must have gone through. But at least I know Sam is alive.

I would never say this to anyone but you, but I think I understand Beth—as well as anyone can who never met her, I mean. Our situations are comparable. She had a life with Al and it was taken away; she waited for years, trying to put together another life that would still have room for him—that wouldn't exclude him or make him feel superfluous once he returned. She had her work and her friends, and her memories.

But I think that eventually she simply wore out. Not her love for Al, but her courage to face those nights. The nights are the worst, Katie. And if I dream about Sam, waking up is the worst of all.

I'm so afraid I'll simply wear out, too. I can't imagine loving anyone else—but loving him so much makes this a specialized hell. Missing him is second nature by now, and that scares me. I don't want to get used to it. I'm ashamed of myself and I hate feeling this way. But I don't have anything but remembering and he doesn't even remember that I exist.

It's better that way. It truly is. I don't think I could stand it if he did remember, because no matter how much we love each other he'd be afraid that it would turn out like Al and Beth—that he'll finally come home and I won't be here.

I will be, not because I'm stronger than Beth or because I love Sam more than she loved Al, but because . . .

"Because I'm stubborn and pigheaded and I won't give up," she said aloud. Her voice sounded suspiciously thick; she took a long swallow of hot tea. "You'll come back. I will *not* believe we'll lose each other forever. Do you hear me, Sam Beckett? I love you and I won't give you up to anyone or anything. Not Time or Fate or Quantum Leaping or even God."

A few silent and thoughtful minutes later, she very calmly erased the last seven paragraphs. She resumed:

> *Everyone here is well, and sends their best to you and Jim and Mom and the kids. The news from the Keck Observatory is incredibly exciting—especially the Beckett Comet! Sam will be so proud when he comes home.*
> *If you can get time off after the Caltech conference, call me and we'll meet somewhere in between—Phoenix or Sedona, maybe? I could use a few days off. Let me know.*
> *Thanks again for thinking of me on my birthday.*
> *Love always,*
> *Donna*

Rising, she walked unerringly through the dimness to the fold-out corner table where she and Sam always ate Sunday dinner. She set the laptop on it, ready to plug into the printer tomorrow morning. The plastic case knocked against something she didn't remember being there.

Her heart stopped, then thudded wildly. Evidence? A change here reflecting a change Sam had made?

Shaking, she fumbled her way to the wall switch and tapped it. The table had sprouted a tall blue vase filled with two dozen yellow roses. A plain card was propped against the vase. She opened it and read:

Happy Birthday, Doña Dulcinea.
I love you.
Sam

CHAPTER
EIGHT

Unable to bear the sight of Alia another instant—
and positive that if he downed another drop of sweet
mead he'd throw up—Sam slipped away into the
trees. He headed for the only refuge he knew: Philip's
tent. Al dogged his heels, mercifully silent.

After untying the flap, Sam walked inside. Al
walked in through the wall.

Smart-ass hologram.

And he was off in Camelot again. Though the cigar
was a poor substitute for a sword, Al played Sir
Lancelot anyway, advancing against the defenseless
rack of chain mail.

"By St. George and the Dragon, that was terrific!
Brave knights vying over a question of honor, challenge to combat—"

Sam lit the Coleman and hefted the ice chest onto
the table, fumbling with the catch. He knew what
Al was doing. He let him do it. Anything to avoid
talking about Alia.

"The only thing missing was the trumpets! *That*
to Lord Rannulf!" The cigar stabbed like a rapier.

Sam opened the lid of the ice chest. "I put the manuscript back right where I found it. See? I knew it would be—"

Right where he'd found it, nestled among the sodas and beers, a bag of Three Musketeers bars, a salami, and a wedge of (what else?) Swiss cheese.

Sam gaped at the fat envelope. "It's here. But—"

"Chivalry to the right of us," Al sang out as he battled the hapless chain mail into submission, "troubadours to the left of us—"

"Al!" He waved the manuscript in—and partially through—his friend's face. "Roger didn't steal it. It's *here*."

"Huh?" Al put the cigar back in his mouth, puffed once or twice, then frowned. "Then what did Cynthia read?"

A wail from the handlink drew his attention. Sam tossed the manuscript onto the cot and opened the briefcase one more time. Philip's notes had to be here. He'd just missed them somehow. They *had* to be here. Besides, searching for them kept him from thinking about Alia.

"Aw, come on, Ziggy! Gimme a break! Sam, you won't believe what she's on about now. Sam! Pay attention."

"I'm listening," he lied, sorting pages like a frantic file clerk after the copy machine's nervous breakdown.

"What Cynthia read really *is* the manuscript that got published. What you've got there is Philip's version."

Sam glanced up from a scrawled column of figures that set his heart thumping until he realized Philip

90

had been doing nothing more vital than calculating his checkbook. "But how? I mean, you said this is the book, and it's Philip's name on the title page. Roger must've stolen and rewritten it, right?"

"Ziggy says it was a collaboration."

"They worked on it together? Those two? Ziggy must be wrong. They can't possibly be—"

"Friends? Sounds weird to me, too, but it's true dish." He read aloud as Ziggy provided data. "They met in the Medieval Chivalry League in '84. Boon companions, drinking buddies—even though Philip's light years ahead of Roger brainwise. Philip got him a better job at a subsidiary of the company he works for—slow down, Ziggy! Cynthia came into the picture in '86, at the Yuletide Frolic. Ooh, I like the sound of that." He paused to conjure the scene. "I'd love to get her and her *orbs* under the mistletoe. . . ."

"I bet you would," Sam muttered. "What you mean is that Philip and Roger fell in love with the same woman, and that was the end of their friendship." How depressingly predictable.

"No, they didn't start arguing until the book got in the way. They'd been playing around with it since '85, just for fun. Lots of swords and battles—real authentic stuff, too, just like I told you. But no romance. Philip wanted a hot and heavy love interest for the Comte de St. Junien, but Roger's a purist."

Sam stared at him, dropping his finger-file of pages gleaned from shaking out old magazines onto the cot. "Excuse me—*Roger*?"

"Look at it this way: does Roger look like he needs any wish fulfillment when it comes to women?"

He had to concede the point.

"They fought about it, in person and on their modems." Al jiggled the handlink, peering at tiny letters marching across the screen. "Philip went ahead and put Alix into the book, using Cynthia as the model. Roger hacked into Philip's computer, decided it was a great idea after all, and wrote his own version. His draft with Cynthia in it is dated four months *after* Philip's. And before you ask, I know all this because it was on Philip's computer disks. He bequeathed his papers and so forth to his company, and Ziggy cracked the archives half an hour ago."

"Did she find anything about the Capacitor?"

"No." Al's lips tightened with disapproval. "Has anybody ever told you that you're a real pain in the ass when you've got a fixation on something?"

Tossing the papers aside, Sam jumped up and began to pace. It was not an entirely satisfactory exercise: three steps, bump into the table, three more steps, bump into the cot.

"Let me get this straight, Al. There are two manuscripts of the same book, one garbage and one great—according to Cynthia, anyway. It has to be Roger's that gets published, right?"

"But Philip's really the coauthor, even if his version *is* stinkola. Whadaya think?" Al mused. "The money?"

"No." Sam shook his head. "He doesn't strike me as the type. He must want the credit."

"With Cynthia," Al agreed. "After all, it was his idea to use her as a character—but once she figures out who Lady Alix is, because she read Roger's version first, she'll think it was all his idea."

"She already knows she's in the book. She just doesn't know who put her there."

Al paused to ponder. "Actually, Alix isn't much like Cynthia at all. They're both beautiful blondes, they both make wind chimes, but other than that . . ." He shrugged. "Alix de Courteney was a woman of her time. A real medieval lady, not a twentieth-century anachronism plunked down in the Crusades."

Sam knew all about being an anachronism. "Meaning she was illiterate, sewed a lot of tapestries, and had lice."

"Yuck."

"If I were Cynthia, I wouldn't be flattered. I'd be insulted."

"Huh." Al puffed at his cigar and flicked an ash onto the Imaging Chamber floor. "You know what? I think both these morons fell for Cynthia only *after* they turned her into Lady Alix. Like the Greek guy who got the hots for that statue."

Sam supplied the names absently. "Pygmalion and Galatea. The original source is Ovid, *Metamorphoses*. George Bernard Shaw adapted the idea in his play *Pygmalion*, which Lerner and Loewe used as the basis for *My Fair Lady*."

And how could he remember that, and not the really important things?

"Yeah—only Alix is on paper, and Cynthia's a real live *girl*." After a brief hesitation, Al finished, "Except Cynthia isn't Cynthia anymore."

There. It was said. They had to talk about it. Sam sank back down onto the cot, taking a pile of briefcase papers onto his knees. "I know," he replied inadequately.

"Ziggy's got no idea where Alia comes from, Sam. There's no record anywhere of a Project like ours. Then again, how much data about Project Quantum Leap is available to anyone with less than a Quad-A security rating?"

"Yeah, but *something* should've shown up. Ziggy never met the computer she couldn't trick, outsmart, or connive into spilling its guts, so I don't understand why—" He broke off in mid-sentence as a terrible idea smote him. "Al . . . could Alia be from farther on in the future? Maybe 2010, 2015—"

"I don't think I like where you're taking this."

"—and somehow they stole the specs, the technology—"

"Sam, I *really* don't like this."

"—*and we didn't even know it?*"

"No," Al said fiercely. "I don't believe it."

"Then how does it happen? Alia Leaps into a particular time and place and person—just like me. There's an artificial intelligence of some kind giving her information—just like Ziggy."

"And she's got a hologram for a partner—just like me." The usually wry and whimsical face had become grim, implacable stone. "No," he repeated. "And I'll tell you why I don't believe it. Project Quantum Leap is unique, Sam, because *your brain* is unique. There's never been even a hint of anyone else working on something like this."

"But that doesn't mean—"

Al ignored the interruption. "So if I believe that Alia's Leaps work just the same way as yours, then I'd have to suspect everybody who ever worked with

94

us. I couldn't trust *anyone*. And I won't live that way."

Sam thought it over. Of the dozens who had helped construct the various components, the dozens more who had knowledge of the Project, and the core personnel who knew almost everything there was to know about it (the last group being the most potentially dangerous), he couldn't think of a single one he didn't trust implicitly.

Then again, how much about them did he truly remember?

No. Al was right. Sam couldn't live that way, either. He had to trust the people who had worked with him to make his dream a reality. They were the very people working to bring him home.

"Yeah," he said softly. "I agree."

Al exhaled cigar smoke and looked relieved. "I guess we'll never know where Alia comes from. But I do know one thing about her. She's your opposite, Sam. She's evil. Just sensing her sends Ziggy into spasms. Keeps saying she's got a bad feeling about this."

Sam took refuge in sorting more papers so he wouldn't have to meet his friend's gaze. "Ziggy's not the only one."

There was a long pause before Al ventured, "What do you remember about last time?"

Her hands on his arms, warm and real.

Her eyes, wide and startled, wild with speculation and a brief flash of fear.

The instantaneous recognition of a kindred spirit, a soul in sympathy with his own. Not love at first sight (he knew how that felt, even if he couldn't

95

remember anything more than a cloud of dark silky hair)—no, not love, but empathy, and compassion, and—

Desire. After the shy excitement of discovery, of revelation that he wasn't alone in this mad dance through Time, he remembered being drawn to her, and her hands drawing him onward.

He remembered, too, how she had raked her own cheek bloody, and screamed, and pointed a gun at his heart.

"Enough," he grated. "I remember enough."

"Well, then—"

"Look, let's give Ziggy something constructive to do so she'll stop worrying about Alia. Get her to work with Philip Larkin. They ought to have a pretty good time—he understands computers, and—"

"If he was okay, I'd say go for it. He's better now, but . . . you know how it is, Sam. Some people go semi-comatose, some go all hysterical. He's the in-between type. He just stands there drinking cappuccino and staring at his reflection. *Your* reflection." Al hesitated, then finished, "I think he sees you as the original White Knight."

"Me?" Sam almost laughed.

"You." Al was giving him a funny look, as if considering Philip's assessment. Sam glanced away, down at the paper in his hands.

And looked more carefully.

Just a scribbled multicolored mess of a diagram. A long blue coil (in crayon, for Pete's sake) ended in braided black lines that disappeared into a gray cube with yellow waves radiating outward. Appropriately obscure scientific notations squiggled their

96

way down the right side of the page. Once, Sam might have known what all of it meant.

But he recognized enough to set his palms sweating.

"This is it, Al. The Larkin Capacitor."

"It is?"

"No, it's not!" he exclaimed, surging to his feet.

"Make up your mind," Al suggested.

"Damn it, this is all wrong! The juice won't flow around corners, there's no cutoff switch—and what's he doing with this gizmo over here?"

"Aw gee, Sam," drawled Al, "I just love it when you talk all technical."

"Scan this for Ziggy," Sam ordered, spreading the childish drawing on the table. The handlink was directed at the diagram. Al scanned. Sam fretted.

Philip Larkin was more than two years away from patenting the Capacitor. Sam didn't remember enough about it to help from this end. It was up to Ziggy, who ought to be able to figure it out, especially if Philip pulled himself together to help her.

(*The White Knight? Me?*)

But what about Alia? What had brought her here? An accident, like last time?

Or had that been an accident? Had they been looking for him, whoever "they" were? If Sam put things right, did she follow after and try to put them wrong again? Or did it work the other way around, and he was fated to sweep up her disastrous debris?

Why maneuver them into that ridiculous challenge? The worst that could happen was that Roger would thump Sam again tomorrow. The weapons didn't have an edge; Roger wasn't out to kill

Philip. So if that was Alia's plan, she was doomed to disappointment.

But she didn't need Roger to kill Sam. She was perfectly capable of doing it herself.

No. She couldn't do it the last time.

Still, between then and now—between that now and this one—what had been done to her? He could still hear her screams as she vanished; he'd thought for a moment that she'd died, told himself she must have. But something else told him she still existed. He'd felt it, denied the feeling, and ordered himself to believe she'd been killed.

Cynthia Mulloy, editor of books and crafter of wind chimes, couldn't matter to Alia. Nor Roger Franks with his particle physics and fiendish backhand (Sam's shoulder still hurt). No, Philip Larkin was the important apex of this triangle, for what he would accomplish in two years' time.

But Sam now stood in Philip Larkin's place. Perhaps he stood in Alia's way.

Until he found out why she was here, all else was wheel-spinning.

If it's not Philip, it's me. There's no reason to think that this time's any different from last—she's been ordered to stop me. Even if she originally Leaped in for Philip, my being here instead changed that.

Whatever happens to me will affect Philip—and therefore the Larkin Capacitor, and therefore me. If Alia kills me, Philip will be stuck in the future, never having invented the Capacitor in the first place—

And if he'd never invented it, there'd be no Quantum Leaping—and I couldn't be here for Alia to kill.

But I am *here. If I* die *here, what happens to Philip?*

Sam figured he ought to be pretty good at playing Temporal Tiddlywinks by now. But there were some things even *his* mind simply refused to wrap itself around. This seemed to be one of them.

His guts told him Alia couldn't kill him. She might try, goaded by her controller, but she was incapable of it. Despite Al's conviction otherwise, Sam knew she wasn't evil. But whatever controlled her Leaps *was*. And that terrible tension between what she was and what she was ordered to do must drive her half-mad at times.

He remembered his last sight of her: body warping into a sick miasma of color, a scream that split his heart—could the penalty for failure have been so hideous and terrified her so badly that this time she *would* kill him?

Would my death truly set Alia free?

An anguished bleat from the handlink snapped Sam's head up. Al was holding the blinking box away from him as if it had just sprouted fangs, talons, and a dragon's forked tail.

"Calm down, Ziggy! It's okay, honey—Gushie, *do* something!"

"What's wrong with her?" Sam asked, alarmed.

"You oughta know," Al accused, frantically pushing buttons. "What you just said set her off like the Bicentennial fireworks off Manhattan! Damn it, Gushie—"

"What I just—oh." He must've voiced the last part, about his death and Alia's freedom. "I didn't know Ziggy cared."

"About you? Gimme a break. It's herself she's worried about. She won't even *consider* the idea that she was never born. The Larkin Capacitor isn't even part of her personal design specs! Okay, honey, take it easy. Sam didn't mean it. He was just—Gushie, settle her down!"

Sam comprehended Ziggy's distress instantly. No Larkin Capacitor, no Quantum Leaping. No Quantum Leaping, no need for Ziggy. It was an intolerable threat to her colossal ego. Well, he couldn't exactly blame her; he'd programmed her that way.

But her ego crisis neatly summed up the difficulty and confirmed Sam's own analysis of what Alia's purpose must be.

The whole point of his own Leaps was to change history for the better. Alia's purpose was just the opposite. Time as it stood now included the Larkin Capacitor. If she changed that . . .

No Larkin Capacitor, no Quantum Leaping.

He kept his thoughts to himself. Ziggy seemed to be feeling fragile, which was scary in a computer with more self-esteem than Henry Kissinger. Working on Philip's notes would be good for her. She was a smart girl when she wasn't having gigawatt hysterics.

Sam's own smarts were leading him someplace very specific. And from whatever path he approached, the destination looked the same.

These past years, and everything I've done during them, would never have happened. I'd instantly go back home—or into oblivion.

Either way, whatever's controlling Alia would win.

CHAPTER NINE

"She's *where?*"

"With Dr. Larkin, Admiral. Dr. Beeks considered it not inadvisable for them to converse."

Al felt worry-wrinkles dig into his forehead. *Not inadvisable* meant that Verbeena had objections but couldn't think up any really good excuses.

"At this hour?" Al asked. "Do you have any idea what time it is?"

"I *always* know what time it is. And you are in error, Admiral. Whereas time is perceived by humans as a subjective experience, it is neither an idea nor a concept but a provable fact. Shall I detail the equations or simply inform you of the hour? If the latter, specify military parlance or vernacular."

Al gave the computer a dirty look.

"I might add that you would have no need to ask me the time if you hadn't left your watch on Tina's dressing table. Again."

"Never mind." He tossed the handlink onto the main terminal board. "I'll be back in a little while."

"Define your terms," the computer requested.

He paused at the control room door and swung around. "What?"

"In the past calendar month, Admiral, you have employed the adverbial phrase 'in a little while' on twenty-seven separate occasions. The period of time was in each case completely different, ranging from 9.62 minutes to 7.58 hours. Common politeness dictates that you define precisely what it is you mean in this instance by 'a little while.'"

"'Common politeness'?" He scowled with suspicion. "Has Gushie been feeding you Emily Post or something?"

"No, Admiral," Ziggy answered. "In my attempt to interface more efficiently with human computers, I am simply requesting information. Being polite is *your* responsibility, not mine."

When Ziggy felt vulnerable, she became pedantic. Considering the gazillion or so subjects on which she was one of the world's leading authorities, he supposed he was lucky she'd chosen manners as her topic tonight. At least she wasn't gibbering anymore.

Still, this was getting a little uppity, even for Ziggy.

"I'll be back *in a little while*," he reiterated. "And it'll take as long as I decide it's going to take. Okay?"

"You needn't get huffy, Admiral."

Al snorted and left. A course at charm school wouldn't hurt that monstrous electronic ego at all.

He dawdled on his way to the Waiting Room. He knew he was dawdling, and did it anyway—until he happened by a certain door.

As smoothly as if he'd stepped on a sensor pad outside a supermarket, the gray door slid open. *Ziggy, you ratted on me!* Al thought, but normal human response made him glance inside anyway.

Verbeena sat at her desk, looking straight at him. She arched her eloquent brows, pursed her luscious lips, and thumbed a button to close the door again.

"Yeah, yeah," Al muttered, lengthening his strides down the hall. "Chronic avoidance syndrome. Heard it all before."

N.B.A. stood for No Bullshit Allowed.

In principle, shrinks made him nervous. Or at least they had until a plain-talking pixie of a therapist guided him to certain realizations regarding himself, and Tina, and Beth. It still hurt even to think his first wife's name, but he found he was no longer quite so emotionally paralyzed by the memories. He could even smile—sometimes—when reminded of her.

Still . . . he would always love her, with the passion of the young man who had married her and the tenderness of the much older man who'd returned to find her gone. He would always believe that what they shared would have grown stronger and deeper—if only they'd been allowed to share it.

Beth. . . .

No, he told himself stoutly, the hurt was not quite so bad. But it would always hurt.

Even so, he had to smile now as he thought of that adamant little dynamo and her wise—if blunt—counsel. Funny, how even though she'd worn Sam's aura and spoken with Sam's voice, Al had never seen anyone other than a tiny woman with a fuzz of hair, never heard anything but a high-pitched soprano and a unique accent.

It was the only time that had happened to him.

At first they'd thought only Sam's consciousness Leaped, and that the body in the Waiting Room really was his. After all, it *looked* like Sam. The working hypothesis had been that Sam's body stayed put while his essence—soul, spirit, consciousness, whatever one was inclined to term it—went elsewhere.

It had shocked the living hell out of them when Verbeena announced that although the body might *look* like Sam's, it wasn't.

Ziggy had commented smugly that she could've told them that, if only they'd thought to ask. Al had threatened to pull her plug. She replied she didn't have a plug to pull; he told her this could be arranged. She finally took the hint and shut up about it.

Only twice had Sam been Sam again. Once his adult self had Leaped into his teenaged self—and the kid in Sam's adult body had scared Al half to death when he'd called him by name. To be expected, Ziggy opined, when the neurons and mesons were identical—just thirty or so years younger—and had merged while passing each other during the Leap. They'd all dithered for days, afraid of what Sam might learn too soon. Fortunately for their collective peace of mind, the kid was distractible: food, an antique Pac-man, the hoop and basketball from his adult self's office, and several IQ tests kept him busy. (Predictably, the test results had been off the scale. Verbeena had spent the next month analyzing the data and writing a paper—"An Essay in Frustration: Comparing the Adolescent and Adult Intelligence Quotient Scores in a Subject Whose IQ Cannot Be Measured"—for some grotesquely esoteric journal, which had rejected her work and snidely suggested she cease propagating fairy tales. She canceled her subscription.)

Once, Sam came home. For twelve hours, he came home.

After that, Donna stopped visiting the Waiting Room.

Sammy Jo (more properly, Samantha Josephine Fuller, Ph.D.) went in when she had time, and Al was pretty sure she reported back to Donna. Al wondered sometimes if the girl had guessed, if she knew it was her father's face she looked at and her father's voice she heard, even though her father wasn't really there.

But until Sam made the Leap during which he and Abigail Fuller made Sammy Jo, she hadn't existed to become part of the project that was responsible for her existence. If ever they'd been unsure about where Sam's body was, the presence of his daughter removed all doubt.

Personally, Al's brain hurt whenever he tried to follow the twists and double-backs of Time, so he avoided it whenever possible.

Although he might dawdle sometimes on his way to the Waiting Room, he never avoided it altogether.

He went in every day. Every day. He stood now in the doorway, watching Philip Larkin use Sam Beckett's long, lean musician's hands to input a 1992 vintage laptop computer. Al had learned by now to look for signs that whoever was in there wasn't really Sam: changes in the angle of the head, the cant of the shoulders, the gestures and grimaces and quirks of expression that were not Sam's.

But every so often someone would do something— usually smile—that was pure Sam Beckett. "Residual physicality," Verbeena called it, just as Sam experienced holdovers while in someone else's body. Right now, for example, Philip Larkin glanced up, brows arching in a manner so like Sam's that Al's neutral smile grew fixed as his jaw tightened. No wonder Donna had stopped coming in. If such moments shook Al, they must torment her.

But tonight she was here. Nearly two in the morning New Mexico time, and she was here.

Al watched her profile, remembering how she'd looked during one of the very first Leaps—a lovely, brilliant, energetic girl of eighteen, years away from the young woman who'd left Sam Beckett at the altar. But things had changed, and the changes were Sam's doing, and the woman who sat talking quietly with Philip Larkin was Donna Alisi Beckett as she was meant to be.

Almost.

For her dark beauty bore a soft patina of sadness. Not bitterness; not Donna. Even though in over four years she had spent only twelve hours with her husband; even though she knew about the other women (not that many—Sam wasn't made that way—but

106

enough to cause acid jealousy in anyone else); even with the loss and the loneliness, there was no bitterness in her. Donna wasn't made that way.

She'd coaxed the whole story out of Al shortly after he'd returned from the past to find her in the control room—part of Project Quantum Leap all along, her brilliance aiding and abetting Sam's genius. Al's own memories had been violently rearranged, and for the first time he experienced a serious shock to his psyche.

Sam's first Leaps had been people whose lives hadn't touched Al's in any way. There were no memories to change. But Donna was different. Seeing her there, worried and tense as Ziggy once more searched through Time for Sam, Al had reacted badly—to say the least.

His last memory of her had been June 4, 1984, the night before the wedding. After the rehearsal dinner he whisked Sam off to a wild bachelor party. After that, nothing. Sam never said her name again. Now, with mind-jarring abruptness, there was an image in his mind of Donna in a bridal gown, miles of white silk cascading to the floor of the Old Mission Chapel in Taos.

In the midst of his confusion, an old rhyme nattered at him: something old (her grandmother's lace veil), something new (Sam's wedding present of small diamond earrings), something borrowed (her mother's pearl necklace), and Al's gift of his own grandmother's handkerchief with blue embroidery tucked into her sleeve. The initials had even been right—*D.A.*, Dorotea Abruzzi, Donna Alisi. He could still remember giving it to her that morning, just before departing the dressing room to stand beside Sam and wait for her to glide gracefully down the aisle . . . .

Except he *hadn't* given it to her, because no one could find her, and he'd stood beside Sam for a solid hour before it became obvious that Donna would not be there. . . .

But here she was, wearing a gold ring on her left hand—the wedding ring Al pretended he'd forgotten, and then honestly couldn't find in any of his pockets, while Sam looked murderous and Donna repressed giggles. . . .

His back pocket, he remembered. He'd put the little velvet pouch containing the ring in his back trouser pocket—good thing he found it, too, or Sam would've throttled him. . . .

More images rushed in, overwhelming him until he staggered both emotionally and physically, unable to make sense of Donna's presence. He backed away, shaking and sweating in a classic case of shock. It was the only time Verbeena ever raised her voice, yelling for Tina and Gushie to help her get him out of there.

In decent privacy, with Verbeena talking him down, he slowly adjusted. New memories fell into their proper places; old ones seeped away. He slept a few hours and woke with his act together. More or less.

Later, much later, Donna confronted him—if a single questioning, worried glance could be called confrontational. So he explained.

All of it. From the whirlwind of meeting, falling in love, becoming engaged, and leaving Sam at the altar, to the boozy English Lit. prof Sam had been when he reunited Donna with her father.

She listened, saying nothing, twisting the wedding ring on her finger. At length, when he finished, she stayed silent for a long while.

Finally, she murmured, "Then the years I had with him, I would never have had at all but for this thing that keeps taking him away from me."

Al cleared his throat. "Yeah, I suppose you could look at it that way."

"Does he remember me, Al? The way we are now, I mean?"

"The first Leap, he didn't even remember his own name. Tina and Gushie are sure it's not because of glitches at this end. It shouldn't happen. He should be able to remember."

"But he can't." She glanced up, dark eyes oddly serene. "It's probably just as well."

"Just as—?" He gaped at her.

"You must never tell him about me. Promise."

"Donna—"

"Promise, Al," she repeated. "There must be a reason he can't remember. If it's not the Project, then something else must be making sure he remembers only what he needs to."

"Something else?" Al choked out. "*What* else?"

"If I knew," she said, suddenly fierce, "I'd tell him or her or it that I'll do anything, if only it will give me my husband back!"

That was the first time he'd considered what role Something—or Someone—else might have in their time-travel experiment gone awry. It had taken quite a while to admit that perhaps, from a certain point of view, it hadn't gone awry at all.

"Al?"

He snapped back to the present with a blink. Donna stood before him, very beautiful and just a little sad. "Just wanted to check on Philip. How's he doing?"

She nodded over her shoulder. Sam's body was now standing at the mirrored table, gazing down. White clothing emphasized the streak of silver in dark blond hair. Al wondered if Sammy Jo might later develop that idiosyncracy of one prematurely white streak. Sometimes she could be so much like Sam. . . .

And after that Leap—the Triple Play, Gushie termed it—they had all found out why. All of them except Sammy Jo. Donna had exacted solemn promises from everyone not to tell. Barring a few "But doesn't she deserve to know?" protests, they had all agreed.

It was the wisest course, until Sam came home. And perhaps it was Donna's wisdom that Al valued most about her presence on the Project. Sam was a mind-in-a-generation; Tina was only a few rungs below him on the IQ ladder; Gushie was a programming wizard; Verbeena nurtured their all-too-human souls. But Donna possessed an honest and gentle wisdom they all needed. Al didn't like to think what they would have done without her. In losing Sam, they had lost their Project Director, main brain, and friend—but Donna had lost her husband. If she could keep on, so could they. In some slice of Time, they *had* done without her. But that memory was mercifully fading now.

"Has Philip come up with anything about the Capacitor?" Al asked.

A slender shoulder lifted, shifting the turquoise silk of her shirt. "He's like Sam—gaps and holes in his memory. Besides, he hasn't even invented it yet, Al. There's not much for him to remember."

He nodded. "How're you holding up?"

"Me?" She frowned slightly, puzzled.

"I've been kind of worried. You haven't been in here for a while."

She met him stare for stare. "No, I suppose I haven't."

So why are you in here now? And at this hour of the night? He couldn't ask.

She saw it in his eyes anyway, and smiled. "Philip Larkin is our best chance yet, Al."

He nodded, knowing this explained only part of it. What Sam—as Professor Bryant—had shown Donna long ago was that it was better to face your fear than to let it rule your life. What Donna feared most of all was abandonment by someone she loved. Renewing her relationship with her father had healed her childhood trauma. She'd been able to trust in Sam's commitment to her; she'd made her own commitment by marrying him instead of abandoning him at the altar.

Only to be herself abandoned.

Twice now, Al reminded himself. Once when Sam first stepped into the Accelerator. And again when Sam did the same to save Al's life.

But this Donna, changed by the changes Sam had made in Time, would never run away. It might have taken her a long while to return to this room, and

111

Al knew it always took courage for her to come in here. But at last she had—to face her sadness and her emptiness by facing yet another stranger who wore Sam's face.

"He came back to me once, Al. He'll come back to me again."

And now Al had to tell her about Alia, who wanted Sam's death.

Halfway through his recital, Donna jammed her fists in the pockets of her jeans and stared hard at the floor. Al finished and waited for her to say something. Anything.

"In a way, I've been waiting for this," Donna said. "You truly think she's there to kill Sam?"

He hated to say it, but she needed to know. "She tried before."

"And couldn't."

"That's no guarantee." He fumbled in a pocket for a cigar, then recalled Donna didn't like the smell and Philip had sneezed for half an hour the last time Al had come in. "We don't know anything about Alia—who she is, who's controlling her, where she comes from. And *when*? Sam brought that up, and scared the hell out of me. Plus we don't know what's happened to Alia since that Leap. *I* thought she'd died. So did Sam."

"No, Al. He might want to believe it, with some part of him that's frightened of her. Dead, she'd be no threat to him. But alive, he might be able to help her. Set her free."

He rubbed the nape of his neck. Muscles were starting to tighten, signaling a tension headache. "Sam and his goddamned rescue complex!"

112

Laughing softly, she moved to stand behind him and massage his shoulders. "Oh, Al! None of us would have him any different, least of all you!"

"Yeah, well . . ." He closed his eyes. "God, that feels good."

For a few moments neither of them spoke. Then Donna said softly, "Thank you for the roses."

He was very glad she was behind him and couldn't see his face. "Sam left instructions, last time he was home."

Her thumbs stilled on his vertebrae, then resumed their soothing motions. "And wrote the card."

"Uh-huh."

"Should I expect the same in June, on our anniversary?"

"I guess." He was terribly afraid she would ask how many cards Sam had written that night while she was asleep. *"Just in case it takes me a little while to get back home again,"* his note to Al had read.

"A little while"—oh God!

"He knew the instant he got here that he'd be going back," Donna said musingly. "Maybe not consciously, but . . . The only way to bring you home was to Leap into you. He was willing to risk the retrieval program on himself, but not on you."

"Donna," he began, then stopped as aching guilt closed his throat.

"Al. How could it have been your fault?" Her voice changed, lighter and almost playful as her fingers probed at his shoulder blade. "You've got a knot the size of a baseball here. I think this is a job for Tina."

The suggestion had definite appeal. But then he opened his eyes and happened to look at Philip Larkin: still bewildered, still afraid, willing to help but unable to do so. In a little over two years, this man would be dead in a completely avoidable accident. Except that maybe by tomorrow, Sam would be dead, quite deliberately, and Philip would never go home to his own Time.

"Ziggy goes into overload at the very idea of Alia," he said.

"I talked with her about it the first time Sam encountered Alia—or tried to." Donna gave Al's shoulder a last pat and took his arm, guiding him to the door. "I have my suspicions, you know, about those nerve cells Sam used in Ziggy. I think they were just that: cells made up of nothing but your and Sam's colossal nerve!"

Al chuckled, pleased to see her smile. "I'd be insulted, if you weren't insulting Sam, too."

Velvet brown eyes blinked wide, dancing with mischief. "Al! That was a compliment!" She gave him a nudge out the door. "Go find Tina."

"I ought to go back and talk with Sam."

"You ought to get some sleep. Or at the very least go to bed." She winked, and the door slid shut between them.

CHAPTER

TEN

Cynthia Mulloy's pale blue tent was instantly identifiable to anyone who knew her League name. Outside, from tent poles and trees and a wooden coatrack, hung a score of her wind chimes. The night breeze teased music from flashing stained glass, toying with fanciful birds, winged angels, and abstract geometric shapes.

Inside, the tent was furnished with things easy to transport in a car: cot and sleeping bag, folding deck chair, card table. The one elegant eccentricity was the Navajo rug on the canvas floor, dark red splashed with blues and greens and yellows.

Scattered across the table were assorted wires, clippers, beads, and bright slices of stained glass edged in lead. A dozen completed wind chimes dangled from the tent struts. Light from at least twenty blue candles—large, squat cubes to tall tapers—glowed from the silent chimes. Fire-thrown shadows refracted down the tent walls and across the slim, pale form of the woman on the bed.

Alia relaxed against embroidered pillows, Cynthia's crystal headdress tangled on the table and Cynthia's blue gown crushed and ignored on the rug. Alia wore an ankle-length shift, tiny cap sleeves decorated with ribbons, hem frothed with lace. Opaque and demure, it was the most innocently unrevealing of garments and she had chosen it precisely for that reason.

A brief tour of Cynthia's possessions had told Alia much about her current host. Everything from the contents of her makeup bag to the partially edited manuscript beneath the cot (a veritable masterpiece of clichés about dragons) indicated that there were two distinct sides to this woman. One was a ruthless professional, the other a profound romantic. After perusal of Cynthia's tent, Alia secretly admired the graceful balance she had struck between her two selves, evidenced by the sturdy practicality of the furnishings and the dreamy profusion of candlelight. Even the nightgown was a clue to character: lovely and lacy, yet coolly comfortable on a warm summer night.

It must be nice, Alia mused, to integrate the facets of one's personality with such easy smoothness. Like a set of the wind chimes: separate pieces of glass turning as the air took each, yet cut from the same pane and tinkling a soft harmony.

Had she not been a hologram, Zoey would have sent all the chimes ringing in a frantic cacophony as she prowled the tent like a caged panther. Alia watched her through a piece of crimson glass. Curious, she thought, how a hologram could exude waves of nervous excitement; one would think that to sense it, the person would have to be physically present. Then again, Zoey's brain and Alia's were linked.

Alia even knew what Zoey was going to say.

"We've got a lot riding on this, Alia. You'd better not go soft on me again."

Predictable. So was Alia's answer—the only one she could give. "I learned my lesson. Lothos made sure of that."

"Please, darling!" Zoey shuddered in her purple leather jumpsuit. "Must you remind me?"

Alia shrugged. She tossed the bit of glass in the air, caught it, tossed it again. The danger of slicing her fingers on sharp edges didn't concern her. She knew what she was doing.

Zoey did not share her confidence. "You're very calm and collected, I must say. And without much reason to be, all things considered. Wasn't seeing him again something of a shock?"

"You warned me he was here." She watched the flight of the crimson shard, slender and curving like a feather lost by some tropical bird. She caught it before it tumbled down into her lap. "I knew where I'd be going before I arrived."

"A very successful scouting trip," Zoey acknowledged with a feral smile. "And this time . . ."

"Mmm. This time." She held the glass to one eye, staring at the candle flames. She could have blown each one out with a soft breath, but Zoey's pacing disturbed the little fires not at all. Zoey was helpless here. She needed Alia to do her work for her.

Lothos's work, Alia reminded herself, and wondered what Sam Beckett's work might be this time. Wondered if stopping him would be enough.

Perhaps it was the medieval milieu she found herself in, but it occurred to her suddenly that Sam Beckett was like a sword blade: strong steel, brightly polished, cleanly edged—a weapon of defense that could slice through her bonds and set her free . . . yet powerful enough to be her death.

Zoey interrupted her thoughts again. "I'm curious, my pet. Whatever made you think of goading them to challenge each other to combat? It was positively inspired!"

"It seemed appropriate to the circumstances." She smiled to herself. "And I thought Lothos would be amused."

"The delectable Dr. Beckett didn't look at all amused." Zoey passed through a wind chime hanging in the center of the tent. No movement, no sound. A ghost would have more effect. But a ghost wouldn't be linked to Alia, a ghost couldn't be the focus of energies that wrapped around her and warped her back and forth in Time—or to a hell that terrified even Zoey.

Alia thought it might be nice to be a ghost. To be dead. Really, truly, honestly dead, instead of being denied the chance to live. It was an intriguing idea, really. Dead, she would be free of all this, and maybe know a little peace.

Zoey gave her none. "That great big gorgeous hulk—Roger, was that his name?—he'll make mincemeat of Sam Beckett tomorrow. I can't wait. All for truth, glory, and honor! Men are deliciously silly, aren't they?"

"It seems very important to them," Alia mused. "Glory and honor. . . ."

"To Beckett, certainly. He believes all those pretty words that mean nothing in the end." She swung round abruptly. "You'd best hope he doesn't drop by tonight, Alia darling. He's bound to ask all sorts of tiresome questions. You can't tell him the truth— and don't think you'll be able to fob him off with lies this time."

Alia repressed a sigh. How she wished Zoey would go away and leave her alone, just for an hour or two of peace.

"What you mean is you're afraid I'll go all teary-eyed if I'm alone with him. Zoey, *darling*, that's exactly what I plan to do."

"What?!" Zoey exploded. "Are you out of your mind? Do you want another fiasco like last time?"

"You said that this afternoon he was feeling terribly sorry for himself." Alia shrugged and said nothing more; let Zoey figure it out from there. She watched the hologram's dawning comprehension through the crimson glass. *Rose-colored?* The touch of whimsy was instantly quelled by reality. *Not roses. Blood. Whose blood, Sam? I bled last time.*

"Yes, I see!" Zoey laughed. "This has definite potential! Alia, do you think we might possibly . . . ?"

"If I were given more time, perhaps." Zoey would never hear the bitter irony of it, that Time to Alia was no gift. Not anymore. "I don't know if he's ready." *Or if he'll ever be—he didn't seem at all tarnished to me.* "No matter what you overheard, his belief is very strong."

"If only Lothos could do something about his partner," Zoey fretted, pacing again. "Losing all contact with home—he'd feel even more isolated, poor dear. And he wouldn't have any projections to help him, either. I'd love to be able to cancel his meddling hologram."

Alia adjusted soft pillows beneath her head. "That might help. But I think the real problem is what he sees when he looks at me. It's very inconvenient to have him recognize me so quickly, Zoey. To see me as I am, not as whoever I've become."

"What a lovely idea! Shall I have Lothos run some scenarios? It does sound fun, fooling Beckett as well as everyone else. I envy you sometimes, Alia."

Yes, Zoey *would* envy her. Alia resisted the urge to laugh.

Zoey prepared to depart, calling up the vortex that would return her to Lothos. She paused, fingers poised like claws over the handlink. "Our darling do-gooder already knows who you are this time. Our job is to make sure there *isn't* a next time."

"I know," Alia replied. "It's just something I've been thinking about. It could be useful for this little encounter."

"I don't understand."

"Just ask Lothos if it can be done. As you say, it'd be fun to have the aura fool Sam, too."

Zoey entered the final code. "I suppose it *was* too much to hope we could convince the nauseatingly good Dr. Beckett to change sides, as it were. See you later, pet."

For a long time after Zoey vanished, Alia watched each candle flame: steady, bright, gleaming like tiny white-gold swords. At last she whispered, "*We*—as if she knows any of the real horror of it."

Rising, she walked slowly around the tent, pinching out candle flames one by one. By the time she reached the last, a tall blue column in a wooden holder on the table, her fingertips were black with soot and her skin was burned. The sting of it was nothing; she knew what real pain was. But it served to remind her of what awaited if she failed again.

She stared into the flame until its image nearly seared her eyes, but what she saw was Lothos, grim and terrible. And Thames, lurking in rainbow shadows, grinning hugely at the supple application of sheer power. Despite Lothos's seeming omnipotence, he needed others to do his work for him. Once, his offer had seemed the way out of a certain kind of hell.

That was before Alia had been taught what hell truly was.

She closed her eyes tight, the candle flame still burning in her mind. Ah, how she wanted to be herself again. Alia, only Alia, whatever her weaknesses, whatever her sins. . . .

But if she could not be herself, she thought it might be just as good to be a ghost. To be dead, and therefore free . . . to find some kind of peace. . . .

Would you do that for me, Sam? Would you kill me, if I told you it would set me free?

He would never understand. He would never wish for death. He wanted his life back. His own life. Whatever his struggles, whatever his doubts, Sam Beckett believed in the rightness of what he did. Whatever his weaknesses, whatever his sins, she could imagine none that could mar that flawless edge or tarnish that bright, bright steel.

Even so, what he wanted and what she wanted intersected at one point. She wanted to be Alia again. He wanted to be Sam.

"We *are* alike," she murmured, and opened her eyes. Finding matches on the table, she relit the wick of a slim blue taper in a hurricane lamp resting on a chair. The pair of flames shone from opposite sides of the tent. "We *do* understand each other, Sam."

She reclined once more on the cot after selecting a dozen pieces of glass from the scatter on the table. She gazed at the two flames through the fragments, one by one, color by color, until he came to her as she had known he would.

CHAPTER

ELEVEN

After Al stepped back through the Imaging Chamber door, Sam fought a brief, inconclusive interior battle. He saw all of it in his head, as if the various players were ranged about on a chessboard, but not as the traditional pieces. Instead, the latest in Medieval Action Figures ($59.95 plus shipping and handling; not sold in stores) came to life in a waking dream.

Philip Larkin and Roger Franks were garbed in gleaming chain mail, their swords, shields, and helmets mirror-bright under a glare of summer sun. Cynthia Mulloy stood in the White Queen's square, resplendent in pink velvet and crystal, holding a thick manuscript. And then there was Alia, looking astonishingly like Joan of Arc (Sam's only reference for a woman in armor—but was she Knight or Pawn?). Behind her in rainbow shadows lurked her controller, centered on the Black Queen's square. Sam himself sat on horseback smack in the middle of the board—and whimsy or self-mockery made noble steed and shining armor white as snow.

Philip and Roger were yelling at each other, striding back and forth in completely illegal moves. Cynthia was swearing with admirable creativity at them both. Alia began an inexorable march from black square to white and then black again, armor chiming with each step, the dark rainbow swirling from the point of her steel lance like a war pennant. Sam heeled his horse first one direction and then the other in an agony of indecision. Should he keep Philip and Roger from skewering each other? Or ride forth to his own private battle with Alia? When the Larkin Capacitor—a blue-black-yellow thing spitting sparks and humming with energy like a million angry bees—materialized and threatened to outflank him, he gave it up and retired from the field.

But sulking in his tent like Achilles was not an option. He could do nothing, decide nothing, without information. So he strode through the campground and arrived at Cynthia's tent, bursting through the blue canvas door flap and fuming with indignation.

Believing himself prepared for anything Alia might be up to, he was totally unprepared to find her dozing quietly on the cot, looking like a gentle white-and-golden angel in a flowing lacy nightdress. Her eyes blinked open: wide, blue, softly drowsy until she recognized him. A corner of her mouth quivered in what might have been a smile. She pushed herself a little more upright on the pillows, and the movements of her body were like silk.

"Sam. I was wondering how long it would take you."

"Why are you here?" he demanded without pre-amble. "No—let me guess. Your artificial intelligence unit—"

"Lothos."

Sam nodded curtly. "Lothos. He's been looking for me, hasn't he? So he could send you."

"Or someone else."

"No, you." He began to pace, boot heels sinking into the lush Navajo rug, scarring the nap. "There's some kind of link between us. I felt it last time, and I can feel it now."

"So can I, Sam." One sleeve slipped a little, revealing a curve of shoulder he remembered as velvet and cream in his palm. He ground his teeth and saw that same tiny smile lift her lips. "That makes you angry, doesn't it? That we're connected somehow. But are you angry with me or with yourself?"

"Just tell me if I'm right. In order for you to get to where I am, the person you Leap into has to be touching me." He was talking too fast, revealing too much tension. But he couldn't slow down or shut up; he had to know. "And when the touching happens, the physical link focuses your Leap. That must be how it happened last time."

"Considering your famous Swiss Cheese Theory, I must be difficult to forget. I'm flattered."

He ignored the jibe. "Cynthia and I didn't touch until that moment—and you were there an instant later. That's how it works, isn't it, Alia?"

"It's an interesting theory," she admitted.

"But that's how it works," he insisted.

"What's important is that we found you, Sam—just as Zoey and I promised Lothos."

"You're here for *me*. Not Philip or Cynthia or Roger. Me."

She nodded, blond hair tumbling around her cheeks. She raked it back, then let her hand fall to her side. "We have that in common this time."

That stopped Sam in his tracks. "What do you mean?"

But he knew. Oh, yes.

"You're here for yourself, too, Sam," she said. "For your own life."

He could hear his own voice saying it to Al: *"This time, it's for me. . . ."*

He took a step back from Alia, treading on Cynthia's discarded blue gown. "What will you do?" he breathed.

"I know who Philip Larkin is—was," Alia corrected herself with another smile, "and what he invented. By the way, compared to Lothos, your Ziggy is quite inefficient."

"I'll tell her next time I see her," he snapped.

Alia shook her head ruefully, as if Sam were a child who stared the answer in the face but was unable to see it. Not his fault, poor thing, that he must be led by the hand. The expression scraped Sam's nerves raw.

"Don't you want to know how I know her name?" she asked.

"I must have told you."

"Did you?"

An overwhelming urge to shake her until her teeth rattled was countered by an equally strong need to find out what the hell she was talking about with that knowing little smile on her

126

face. The conflicting emotions effectively paralyzed him.

"You've asked your Ziggy about *me*, haven't you?" she murmured.

"You—" He choked on it.

Lothos knew about him. That "article on that crazy guy at M.I.T.," a dozen more articles and interviews—hell, a *hundred* more, accessible to anyone who could read—oh God, she'd have access to all of it. All the things Al wasn't allowed to tell him. All the things that haunted him by not being there.

> *Yesterday upon the stair*
> *I saw a man who wasn't there*
> *He wasn't there again today. . . .*

Alia probably knew more about him than he remembered about himself.

And suddenly it was a horrible temptation to ask her.

All the questions he asked about other people at the beginning of a Leap, she could answer about him. Who Sam Beckett was, what he had done and when, where he'd lived and studied and worked—his family, friends—was he married? A father? (Somehow, the answers were *yes* and *no* simultaneously; had he done something in a Leap or Leaps to alter his own history?)

There was so much he didn't know. So much he needed to know. Just something as simple as the color of his eyes.

"I know you, Sam." Alia's voice; he listened in agony. "I know where you got all those doctorates, your favorite food, your mother's maiden name, that you played baseball—"

He could hardly breathe for the pounding of his heart. She knew—she had access to endless information about him—she could tell him anything and everything about his life.

But at what price?

"Basketball," he said with an effort. "I was on the basketball team—"

"Yes," she replied, nodding. "But you also played baseball."

"So does every kid in the United States," he managed. "Easy enough deduction, Sherlock."

"Ask me, Sam," Alia suggested softly. "Ask me anything."

Just one thing—surely it wouldn't hurt to ask just one—

No.

Sam met her gaze with an effort. "You could tell me anything for an answer, and I'd never know if it were true or not."

She gave a quiet sigh. "You may or may not believe that I know all about you, Sam, but that doesn't really matter."

"What *does* matter, then?"

"If you'll ever see home again."

His muscles spasmed involuntarily, and he knocked into a set of wind chimes. The noise jangled his already shaky self-command. "Is that why you're here? To keep me from going home?"

"Oh, Sam!" Her brief laugh was almost pitying. "Don't you see? I don't even have to try."

"What the hell does *that* mean?"

"Only that we'll just keep running into each other . . . from time to time." She smiled again at the wordplay.

"You and Lothos will keep hunting me down," he accused, "trying to stop me from doing what I have to do. Can't you think up a better way to spend your time?"

"Time isn't ours to spend." She sat up, staring down at her hands—clasped as if at prayer. The twinned candle glow and refracted stained-glass light shone off her gold-and-whiteness, off the shards of color in her lap. "Think of it, Sam. Think about how I find you, and what that means. You don't dare touch anyone during a Leap again, for fear I'll be there the next instant. You don't dare let anyone touch *you*. Not for love . . . or loneliness . . . or even to save a life."

"I'm not afraid of you."

But did he say it to convince her—or himself? He hurried on, not wanting to examine that question any more than he wanted to be tempted with what she might or might not know about him. (An exquisite face, a cloud of dark hair, being so much in love that he wanted to laugh and dance with the crazy joy of it every time he looked at her—)

"You're not evil," he insisted. "Lothos is. Whatever it is he makes you do to people—you don't have to obey him, Alia! You can break free, you don't have to be a pawn—"

"What about you?" she countered. "Can you break free? You're as trapped as I am. Neither of us will ever get home. All we have is each other."

"You've got Zoey," he managed.

129

"And you have your friend Al," she answered readily. "Your only contact with home. Someone else you can never touch." Alia bit her lip suddenly. "What do Al and Zoey know about it, Sam? *They* go home whenever they like. *They* look in a mirror and see their own faces. *They* don't have to be afraid that they'll never see home again."

He knew what she was doing. She was pushing, pushing, making him doubt, playing on his weariness and loneliness and resentment, appealing to the dark despair in him exactly as he once appealed to any light left in her.

Quick study.

"Sam . . . do you remember *you*? What you look like? Do you even know the color of your own eyes?"

Damn her—*damn* her! She could get to him and she knew it. *He* knew it. After all, it was the same technique he'd used on her. But full awareness of what she was up to didn't make this any easier to hear.

"I can't remember me." Her voice was a brittle whisper, edged in pain that cut into him, too. "I can't remember my own face."

"Alia—"

"You get tired, Sam. Just like me. You've told me so. But don't you ever get angry? Don't you ever want to scream that you've had enough? There are times when I—" She shook herself, raking both hands back through her hair. "I *hate* what's been done to me, Sam! All the things I endure at Lothos's whim—all I want is—"

"To go home." He heard himself finish it, his voice as bitter as hers.

"Is it so much to ask?" she pleaded, as if he could fulfill her wish. "To be myself again? To be *Alia*, not some stranger—to see *my* face in a mirror again?"

Sam took one step back, then two. These were his words, his feelings—

"Stop it," he breathed.

With swift grace she rose. Glass pieces tinkled to the rug. Sam flinched at the sound, backed into another clanging chime, flinched again. Alia was simultaneously dejected and defiant: shoulders slumped and chin lifted, blue eyes filling with tears of rage and grief. Real tears? Yes. But—real emotions? He thought so; the places where he and she were the same ached in empathetic understanding. But did she use her genuine fear and sadness the way Roger and Philip had used Cynthia's blond hair and blue eyes to create a character that wasn't Cynthia at all?

Her hands reached tentatively for him, then fell helplessly to her sides. "Only you and I can understand this, Sam. We're the only ones who know how it feels. Yes, we're linked—but do you know how strongly, and why?"

God, she was good at this. Very, very good. He wondered what Lothos would do to her if she wasn't— and decided he didn't want to know.

"I'm sure of just one thing, Sam." The tears spilled down her cheeks, shining like scars by candlelight. "You've helped so many other people—people you don't even know—and I know that somehow, some way, you'll be able to help *me*. We're linked for a reason. I have to believe that it's because you can set me free." She bit her lips together, then burst

131

out, "You're the only one who can!"

The words leaked from his lips like blood from a stone. "By . . . my death?"

"No!" she exclaimed, and continued quickly, feverishly. "Zoey said killing you could be my way home. But she was wrong, Sam. *You* were right—if I destroyed you, I'd be destroying myself."

Does that work both ways? he thought, a shiver running through him.

"You're me and I'm you, Sam Beckett. We know the same weariness, the same emptiness—we feel the same anger and resentment. We both want to go home. Just to go home. And they won't let us. Ever. We're too useful. Too good at what we do. But we never chose to do it, Sam—they chose for us! And they'll never let us go!"

She was right, and yet he knew she was so wrong—she *had* to be wrong. He didn't know what he felt anymore. He backed into the tent corner, chimes clanging and clamoring all around him, a chair toppling when his awkward foot caught at it.

"Alia—no—that's not—"

She looked bizarrely innocent in the lacy shift, blue eyes brimming. She held out her hands. They trembled, frail as captive frightened birds. He saw then how truly fragile she was—poised precariously between stark terror and desperate loneliness, between Lothos' malign imperatives and the simple human need to be herself. One day, perhaps soon, she would lose her balance.

For now, whatever had been done to her and with her, there was still something left in her eyes of

132

whatever she had been before Lothos. The *something* he had reached in her last time. But if they were mirror images, then he could also see himself in her eyes. She was a reflection of what he might become, should fear and loneliness and anger overwhelm him.

"They'll never let us go home," she whispered. "You're my only home now, Sam. I'm the only person you can touch."

"Alia . . ."

She flinched. "I—I'm the last person in the world you'd want to touch, aren't I?" she said, her voice a mere quiver of breath. Her fingers clutched the pristine whiteness of her nightgown, twisting the material. "But—Sam, don't you see? *You don't dare touch anyone else!*"

Before he knew it he was gripping her shoulders—one of them bare and pale and velvety in his palm—and she was looking up into his eyes as tears rolled like liquid crystals down her cheeks.

"Alia—it doesn't have to be—I don't know how, but we can do something, we have to be able to *do* something!"

"How? When? Do you know what Lothos does to me when I fail?"

He shook his head mutely.

"And even after he's done with me—" She shook briefly, a clenching of every muscle in her body, and he believed that the horror in her eyes was genuine.

"Don't think about it," he said. Probably the stupidest thing he'd ever said in his life.

Her shining head bent, and her voice was small and defeated. "I'll always come back, Sam. Your

133

touch will call me to wherever you are in Time. You can't escape me any more than I can escape you. And neither of us can escape what's been done to us."

"I don't believe that. I *can't*." Hoping he sounded more certain than he felt.

She broke free of his grasp, knuckling her eyes like a little girl. "We're trapped. Forever. All we have is each other. I've accepted it. Perhaps you should, too."

"No. It's not true!"

Swinging around to face him, she cried, "So you cling to your delusion that one day you'll go home? What have they done to *you*, Sam, that you won't see what's so obvious? Why won't you believe me?"

"Because . . . because if I did—"

He didn't dare finish the thought, not even in his own mind. He took the only escape open to him—physical escape, fleeing into the night.

"Sam!"

He was gone.

Alia collapsed back on the cot, wiping her eyes. "Well," she said aloud, furious at the way her voice quivered. "If Zoey were here, she'd ask me how much of that I actually believed. . . ."

Quite unaccountably, she put her face in her hands and began to weep.

CHAPTER TWELVE

Sunday morning, and the campground was abustle. Most people were up early, toting ice chests and tables, cots, chairs, and garment-bagged costumes to the parking lot a quarter of a mile away, getting a jump-start on their packing before the long drive home. But no one even considered leaving before the epic joust.

Zoey regarded all this activity with a shudder of distaste. "Sunday morning after a Saturday night banquet—how *can* these people be up at this hour and look so bloody cheerful about it?"

"It's nearly nine." Alia had been awake since dawn. She shook out her dress—a yellow cotton skirt over a white petticoat, with a green laced bodice and blouse, rather like an inverted buttercup—and kept walking through the tiny village of collapsing tents. There was much chatter about the Fair, which Alia had not yet seen; the crafters would be the last to tear down their stalls, hoping for last-minute sales. Perhaps, Alia thought, if she led Zoey to a place where a conversation with thin air would be remarked on,

135

Zoey would give up and go away.

No such luck.

"You must have said something perfectly lethal last night, darling," Zoey rattled on as they reached the double row of booths. "When I stopped by our hero's tent he was looking quite bleary."

"Was he?"

"It's scarcely fair," she added, pouting. "He's even appealing as a haggard insomniac—although one could wish for a more interesting reason for lack of sleep." She paused, surveying the replica of a medieval fair. "How . . . quaint. Quite the thing, if one is into rustic charm."

Someone offered a "Good morrow, my lady!" to Cynthia. Alia smiled back. The booths ranged from authentic-looking wooden structures to folding tables disguised with cloth, but all were bright and lively and crammed with goods. She paused to finger a length of handwoven wool and admire the cloaks draped on hangers for display.

"Best prices all year, Lady Cyndaria," said the dealer, who was winding nubby scarlet yarn into a ball. A small loom was set up at her side, a piece begun in vivid blues. "That lavender cloak you like hasn't sold yet."

Peering into the booth, Zoey said, "*That* hideous thing? Now, the hunter-green one with all the gold embroidery, that's not half bad. And just my color, too."

"I might be persuaded to knock the price down," the crafter suggested.

Alia smiled again, shaking her head, and moved on.

"Ribbons and laces!" came the call down the row. "Last chance before Harvest Fest! Ribbons, laces, and fine embroideries!"

"I don't think you're paying attention, darling."

She glanced at Zoey, brows arching, and made a small gesture with one hand to indicate the scores of shoppers around them.

"Jeweled goblets and silver tankards!" sang out another vendor. "Fine pewter loving cups!"

The hologram sighed. "Oh, very well. I suppose you have to play to the rabble. My point is that Beckett will be too exhausted to do himself much good against Mr. Muscles. So everything has the potential to work out just fine. Roger-Rannulf will get the money and the girl—neither of which he'll keep for long—Philip will drink himself into an automobile wreck, and nothing will have changed." She paused. "But that's only our worst-case scenario."

"Mmm," Alia responded absently. She knew very well the "best case" Zoey had in mind.

She walked on, examining leather goods, embroidery, ceramic platters, brass goblets, handwoven scarves. Beautiful work, all of it; the crafters were not only caring but talented. It was with genuine delight that she stopped at a wood-carver's booth, where his cunning little wooden toys enchanted her. There were wry-faced monkeys whose arms and legs moved, and gaily painted birds with flapping wings, and marionettes of all descriptions. What caught her fancy, though, was a white unicorn. Seeing her interest, the crafter named a price. She shook her head, but couldn't resist touching the flowing silver

137

mane, the delicate spiral horn painted gold.

"It looks like it belongs on a carousel," she said wistfully. "I remember when I was a little girl—"

"Unicorns," Zoey reminded her with poisonous sweetness, "are for the pure, the innocent, and the virginal."

Blindly, Alia left the booth, not even hearing the wood-carver call out a lower price.

Zoey strolled along beside her, walking with perfect unconcern through a young man strumming a mandolin. "Bearing in mind that Boy Scout Beckett is the main objective now, and not this absurd love triangle, I'm waiting to hear you explain your suggestion of this morning. And I might as well remind you again that what you're asking has never been done before."

"Pomanders!" cried a girl as she strolled the aisle. "Sweet to the nose, studded with cloves—fresh pomanders!"

Zoey was momentarily intrigued by the items on the shoulder-slung tray. Stuck on the ends of short wooden handles, some beautifully carved and some plain as popsicle sticks, were oranges, lemons, and limes sporting complex patterns of clove buds. Alia's nose twitched at the scents of citrus and spice, threatening a sneeze. She took refuge at a booth of glassware.

The sets of wind chimes, strung in a long row above the plates and bottles and goblets, looked familiar. Alia brushed fingertips across one of Cynthia's creations to set it dancing, and thereby attracted the proprietor's notice. He completed a sale and turned to her, all smiles.

"Your chimes are very popular, Lady Cyndaria. I've sold four just this morning."

"Have you?"

"And the promise of another, if Sir Guthwulf loses his bet with his lady on today's joust."

Alia didn't ask who Sir Guthwulf would be rooting for.

"By the way, Lady Godwyn asks if you'd trade for the blue set. Your choice of her embroidered purses. She does very fine work."

"Godwyn?" Zoey echoed. "How revolting."

Alia pretended to examine the blue chimes as if estimating their value in a trade. "Please tell her ladyship I'll think about it."

"As you wish." He hesitated, then said in a softer voice, "Cynthia, this thing with Phil and Roger—"

She stiffened her spine and dared him with her eyes to say more. He wisely turned to attend another customer.

"Isn't it odd?" Zoey commented. "Nobody else has asked. But I suppose they're all buzzing with it out of your hearing."

"Probably." She'd noticed some odd looks on her way through campground and Fair. Had Zoey not been a hologram invisible to everyone else, Alia would have attributed the looks to the vivid emerald jumpsuit and thigh-high purple leather boots. But it was true enough that no one had broached the subject of the joust.

She stopped for a moment at the soap-maker's at the end of the aisle. The oblongs pyramided on the counter smelled of violets and lavender and sandalwood and cinnamon, and this time Alia did sneeze.

The vendor cast her an amused, apologetic smile.

"Watch out for the potpourri booth across the way, Lady Cyndaria. Worse on your hay fever than rag-weed!"

Alia smiled back and thanked her, then crossed slowly to the other row of booths, murmuring to Zoey, "You say what I'm asking has never been done. Are you also saying it's impossible?"

"You know very well there's hardly anything Lothos can't do."

"Fresh and hot! Griddle cakes and fruit!"

Alia had eaten nothing since the previous evening. Following the voice, she ignored Zoey's rebuke in favor of potential breakfast. Pancakes sizzled in frying pans atop two small hibachis; bowls of cold sliced fruit and steaming compotes awaited on the counter.

"That smells wonderful!"

"Don't be cruel, darling, you know I love crepes!"

"I'll have one, please. Thank you, good sir." She handed over money from the purse at Cynthia's belt. Paper plate and plastic fork were presented, and a moment later a thin pancake slid into position. She piled on hot blueberries and cold peaches, folded the crepe, and sprinkled powdered sugar lightly over the top. She kept walking as she ate, emphasizing the enjoyment for the secret pleasure of irritating Zoey—who was practically salivating even as she resumed her lecture.

"I'll admit that theoretically, it's possible. We're already focused in on this place and time, so it's not a matter of searching at random. It would be a terrible strain, though."

Surprise betrayed Alia into speech; no one paid her any mind, for someone had begun to play a dulcimer in the next booth, thereby attracting a small crowd. "When has my comfort ever been a consideration?"

"A strain on Lothos, not you! He's not especially thrilled by this wild plan of yours."

Alia finished her breakfast and threw plate and fork into a trash can. "Lothos isn't here," she said, voice low and tense. "*I* am. This is *my* assignment, Zoey. I make the plans and I take the responsibility. Does Lothos want Sam Beckett to win?"

"I take it that's a rhetorical question." Zoey blinked suddenly, then smiled in purest pleasure. "Well! Will you look at that!"

The booth was one of the more elaborate at the Fair, perhaps indicating greater prosperity. A wooden awning spread wide, sporting a carved sign featuring crossed silver swords above a golden anvil. All across an expanse of crimson velvet counter and slung from support struts was as impressive a collection of steel weaponry as ever was displayed in a medieval baron's great hall.

It was the real stuff, too—foot-long daggers, broadswords etched with runes, massive claymores, wood-handled pikes with blades wider than a man's spread palm, slim poniards, gleaming battle-axes, even a great curving scimitar. All the weapons were whetted to a hair-splitting edge, and all of them could kill.

A young man in ridiculous scarlet tights and a blazing yellow tunic stood several paces off, hefting a strange weapon as if to test its weight. At the end of a wooden handle were eight inches of thick chain attached to a sphere studded with thick spikes. These were painted red, as if blooded. The man cast an eye at the watchful sword smith, then began to whirl the iron ball overhead. Around and around at the end of the chain it turned, gathering velocity with a sinister hissing sound.

"What a gorgeous little toy!" Zoey exclaimed.

"What is it?" Alia asked softly.

"A morningstar," Zoey replied, eyes alight as the spikes thudded into a tree. "Named for what's at the business end. I really was born into the wrong time, you know. . . ."

"I thought Thames was the one with the medieval fixation."

"Oh, him!" Zoey waved a dismissive hand. "Show him a torture chamber and he's perfectly blissful. Personally, I find medieval weaponry much more elegant. The modern world has forgotten so much by way of really creative killing."

The sword smith was scowling. "Daniel!" he called. "That's enough! Put that thing down before you brain somebody with it!"

"Luscious idea," Zoey sighed.

Daniel pried the star from outraged tree bark. "Sorry," he said, polishing red spikes with his fingers before replacing the weapon on the counter. Alia thought he looked a little shaken at the unexpected power of iron and wood—as well he might. Forget the damage of impact; the look and sound of the thing were threat enough.

The sword smith returned to his conversation with another customer, a man of about fifty wearing sober brown with a heavy silver chain of office draped around his shoulders. "Now, this broadsword has an honest edge to it, Lord Duncan, as with all my wares. You may display it on your person or on your wall at home, but—"

"Don't unsheathe anywhere near the tourney field, or I'll be kicked out of the League. I know the rules, Master Padraic. I helped write them, fifteen years ago. Wrap it up."

Another morningstar lay at rest on the crimson counter. *For display only* . . . Alia mused, fingers tracing the smooth wooden handle, caressing the spiral carving that had been painted bright blue. The spikes looked as if they'd been dipped in gold. After a moment she met Zoey's gaze. And smiled.

"What are you—" Zoey peered more closely at Alia's face. "Why, I do believe you're looking positively fiendish, my pet."

Master Padraic and Lord Duncan were engaged in carefully swathing the broadsword in yards of black cloth. Alia kept her voice soft just the same. "When I give the word, Zoey. Make sure Lothos is ready."

"You'd better explain what for, first!"

"Later. Master Padraic?"

He turned, an impressive sheaf of bills in one hand. "Lady?"

She used Cynthia's admittedly delightful smile to excellent effect. "I don't suppose I could interest you in a set of wind chimes unless they were bound in solid gold."

He made a leg and grinned. "Silver, if the assurance of your smile came with them! I assume you're

143

looking for a gift for today's victor?"

"Precisely."

"Sword? Dirk? Belt knife?"

"That." She pointed.

A brief haggling session later, Master Padraic rummaged in the back of the booth for cloth to wrap her purchase in. As she untied Cynthia's purse to pay for a type of weapon last used in combat over five centuries ago, she murmured, "Have a little faith, Zoey darling."

CHAPTER THIRTEEN

In point of fact, Sam had gotten some sleep. About fifteen minutes' worth.

B.Q.L., he'd had several methods of courting slumber. Attempting a proof of Fermat's Theorem, which had frustrated mathematicians for centuries, had been a favorite for years. After it was solved in 1993, he'd either run through the proof in his head or turned to various alternatives: calculating the probable number of Earthlike planets in the Andromeda galaxy, listing in alphabetical order every song ever recorded by the Beatles, or proposing possible solutions to the linguistic mysteries of Linear A.

Nowadays his choices were limited. Sometimes he couldn't remember the name of the theorem, let alone the proof; he usually forgot one or more of the criteria for the evolution of carbon-based life; he was never sure if the Beatles had ever recorded a song beginning with J; and recalling even the symbols of the ancient Minoan language was iffy at best.

On the night of July 11, 1987, he came damned close to counting sheep.

Considering there was another sword fight with Roger in the offing, Sunday promised to be a rerun of Saturday, only with even less rest. Whatever the Leap immediately previous to this one had been like, Sam's body was positive it had not involved a whole lot of lying down in a bed with eyes closed.

(A voice drifted past in memory—*"You do so snore, Sam Beckett!"*—with the impression of a riotous pillow fight; but when he reached for it there was nothing to grasp except a bewildering image of I. M. Pei's glass pyramid at the Louvre. So he'd visited Paris at some point in his life—or had it been somebody else's life? No, it had been his own, because Al had mentioned something about going to Paris "again." Whatever *that* meant.)

Although this particular Leap might be lacking in blissful slumber, at least the food was good. Sam was at the picnic tables in time for a breakfast that was the veritable definition of Cholesterol Heaven: scrambled eggs with Tillamook cheese, crisp fried bacon, fresh-baked biscuits slathered in butter, and home fried potatoes. Sam wolfed the meal, washing it down with honeyed tea, and finished with a bowl of sliced peaches half-crusted with sugar. He was going to need the energy, and soon; the herald had informed him that the joust with Lord Rannulf was set for just after the parade of ducal colors.

Terrific.

"Spent the whole night glowering at that diagram, didn't you?"

146

He didn't even glance at Al on the walk back to Philip's tent. "Not all of it."

"Huh," was the skeptical reply. "Ziggy's throwing projections at us like Orel Herschiser. If Roger wins the joust, the book gets published, but Cynthia doubts him just enough to keep from marrying him. Philip invents the Larkin Capacitor—"

"And kills himself doing it."

"Well . . ."

Sam finally looked at him. The admiral was fittingly dressed for the momentous medieval occasion: dazzling white shirt with plackets, cuffs, and collar embroidered in twining green ivy and scarlet flowers; sky-blue slacks and matching bow tie; silver mesh belt with a massive buckle cast in the shape of a rampaging dragon. Rather than the appropriate boots, however, he wore white huaraches. Sam envied him the comfort. Philip's boots were a half-size too small, and Sam's feet were killing him.

He also wore Philip's tourney gear of trousers (buttons, no zipper), shirt (more itsy-bitsy laces), and sword belt. The padded tunic and chain mail were still hanging on the rack within the tent, along with the helmet. Sam had thought about doing a few practice runs to learn how to get it all on and off, then decided he'd only get stuck in it and spend the rest of the morning sweating.

Still, as he had contemplated the gleaming steel by the light of the lantern in the wee hours, he began to understand how Philip could lose his shyness when protected by this quite literal armor. Judging by the collection of tin disks that betokened his jousting victories, Philip was a real tiger when in his Sir Percival suit.

In a way, it was rather like what Sam did with every Leap: subsume parts of himself in someone else, wear someone else's face and body and characteristics for a little while. Except that Philip did it by choice.

"We never chose to do it, Sam—they chose for us!"

He banished Alia's voice and went inside Philip's tent. The chain mail stood patiently in a corner, waiting for Sam to fill its emptiness: *Bring me to life, and I'll protect you.* The crayon drawing lay on the table, also waiting for Sam: *Bring me to life, and I'll take you home.*

Alia waited, too. But life or home or protection were not among the things she could offer.

Sam dragged the chair out into the morning sunshine. Silently, calmly, he sat down to polish the sword. "The only advantage to staying awake all night," he told Al, "is that she didn't get the chance to sabotage anything."

"But she could've gotten to Roger's stuff."

"Switched swords, you mean? Given him one with an edge on it?"

"Or loused up his mail or helmet or something."

That hadn't occurred to Sam. He'd been so preoccupied about Alia in relation to himself that he'd forgotten about what she might be planning for Roger. "So he'd be injured or—no," he said, abruptly certain. "He's too good a fighter not to check his equipment before every joust." He rubbed a smudge from the steel with his thumb, turning the sword this way and that to catch the sunlight. "What other

148

cheery news does Ziggy have?"

"If *you* win the joust, Cynthia will publish Roger's version anyway, he'll keep writing, and Philip and Cynthia will get married and do the happily-ever-et-cetera bit."

Sam rested the blade across his knees and plied a soft cloth down its length. It was a lovely thing, as swords went, with a pattern of oak leaves etched into the steel and a dozen seed-sized opals studding the hilt. Philip had paid a lot of money for this weapon, and knew how to use it.

"What about the Capacitor?"

"Oh, don't worry. It gets invented." Al's voice was sour with disapproval.

"When?"

He gave a shrug. "Not until '92."

Sam didn't remind him they'd bought the rights to it in '91. Installation had smoothed out a lot of difficulties, taking at least a year off the Project's completion date.

What he needed to know, he was allowed to remember.

"At least it *does* get invented," Al went on. "And Philip lives, and he and Cynthia are very happy, and—"

A sudden raucous *mroww* made Sam jump half-way out of the chair. The cat was gorgeously Siamese, wearing a blue collar exactly the shade of her slightly crossed eyes. She paced the ground before him, yelling another coloratura demand for Sam to stop whatever useless thing he was doing with his hands and perform the infinitely more essential honor of petting her. Obedient to a

149

lady's demand, he reached down to scratch her pewter-colored ears. "Wonder where Cynthia is right now."

"Wherever it is Alia's victims go when she Leaps into them."

Sam shook his head. "Her only intended victim is me, Al. I'm the one she's here for." He looked reflexively down at the hand she'd touched, that had touched her. How much of what she'd said had been honest? How much had been deliberately designed to shake him to his marrow?

How long before her shaky balance was completely lost?

The cat evidently found Sam's technique deficient. She fixed on Al as a superior source of supply and padded lithely over, purring like a 747 just prior to takeoff. She leaned against Al's leg—and fell over with a yowl of surprise. A try at marking him with her cheek yielded the same result and an even louder protest. Sam watched, smiling in spite of himself, as the peeved Siamese took a quick swipe at Al's pant leg with all claws extended. She missed, of course.

"Sorry, sweetheart," Al apologized.

She had not yet given up. Wriggling down into attack mode, she pounced on his shoe. And again. Frustrated, she backed off, arched, hissed, and spat at him before stalking off with regal disdain.

"You do have a way with women," Sam observed.

"Speaking of which, how'd you do with Alia last night?"

"How'd you—" He stopped, cursing himself for the slip. Naturally Al knew Sam had been to see her; Al knew Sam.

The admiral examined the glowing tip of his cigar. "So? You still think she's a helpless little pawn?"

Sam didn't much care for his tone. "You don't understand her."

"And you do." It wasn't quite a question.

He polished the opal chips with fierce concentration. They caught the sunlight and flung it back in fire that reminded him of the chaotic rainbow enveloping Alia just before her disappearance last time. And that led to memory of her terrified screams.

What did Lothos do to her when she failed?

Al wouldn't let up on him. "Kindred spirits?" he suggested.

"If you want to call it that."

"Don't make me laugh. What'd she tell you last night? She do a poor-pitiful-me act? Or did she put the moves on you again?"

"I don't want to talk about this, Al," Sam warned, keeping a tight rein on his temper.

"Too bad," he said without sympathy. "Because we're gonna *keep* talking about it until you realize she's out to kill you. Anybody with an IQ higher than room temperature could figure it out."

"She *can't* kill me! Hasn't that gotten through to you yet? We're opposites. Without me, Alia couldn't exist."

"And you think the opposite holds true, too, don't you? That if she dies, you'll disappear?"

Sam clenched his jaw shut and rubbed a non-existent speck of rust from the sword blade.

Al exploded. "That's the stupidest goddamned thing I've ever heard you say! And you didn't even have to *say* it!"

"What do you want me to do, Al—run her through with my sword and see if the hypothesis is correct? That as opposites we cancel each other out?"

"At least you admit that she's evil."

Sam's head jerked up, his eyes blazing. "I *don't* admit any such thing! If she's the Devil, then that makes me God—and I don't qualify for the job!"

"You know damned well which side she's on, Sam!"

"She's nothing more than a tool." *Just like I am,* hung unspoken in the space between them. "Lothos is the evil here, Al. He controls her, he sends her through Time, he gives the orders—what choice does she have but to carry them out?"

"And that's why you're like her? Neither of you has any choice?" Al jabbed the handlink furiously. "When you start using that so-called genius brain of yours again, give me a call. I'm outta here."

Sam glared at the place the glowing rectangle had been, then looked down at the sword once more. His fist was painfully clenched around the hilt. In a short time he would be wielding this shining blade against a man who had not the slightest clue what was really going on here.

The Crusaders had used swords much like this one, believing with a rapacious faith that they fought on the side of God and goodness and right. Thus they had slaughtered innocents by the millions, and been slaughtered in their turn.

"Hello, darling!" Zoey caroled gaily as she popped in without warning, as usual. "The court is assembling—absolutely wild with excitement, and betting ten-to-one against Sir Percy—and that riciodulous herald person is about to blow his silly lungs out on that trumpet."

"I'm almost ready." Alia had no notion of how to arrange a wimple, and so had placed the silver-and-crystal cap of last night on her hair. Perhaps it would shock the locals, outrage some custom of modest and seemly dress. She didn't much care. Today everyone would be staring at her—at Cynthia—anyhow, at least until the joust began. "Is Lothos ready? What does he say about my plan?"

"Exactly what he's been saying ever since you proposed it: interesting, possible, but difficult."

Bending to look in Cynthia's mirror, hung from a tent pole and about three inches too low for Alia, she tucked stray wisps of hair behind her ears. "What about the other problem? The aura?"

"Oh, didn't I mention that earlier? Lothos is perfectly fascinated. He and Thames have been discussing it all night." She retied the emerald scarf of her jumpsuit, making an ascot of it as she talked. "The theory so far is that because with the present configurations you and Beckett can see each other as who you really are, the opposite will probably hold true. Fix your mascara, pet. It's flaking."

"So if Sam *can't* see me, I won't be able to see him either?" Alia frowned, wiping a tiny dot of brown from below her eye. "That's not what I had in mind, Zoey. That's no help at all!"

"You'll have to work with what Lothos gives you. It was tough enough convincing him even to consider this other little trick. Thames was—and still is—skeptical."

153

Straightening, Alia caught up a length of yellow chiffon and draped it from her elbows. "Thames," she said acidly, "has all the imagination of a gerbil."

Zoey smirked. "My, what a generous assessment! I'd have chosen something a bit lower on the evolutionary scale."

After one last glance around, Alia started for the tent door. "I'm ready. I hope you and Lothos are."

"Alia, darling, this—"

"Had better work, I know. I know!" Alia interrupted impatiently. "Come on."

CHAPTER FOURTEEN

Quantum Leaping can be seen as a gigantic game of Let's Pretend—"from a certain point of view."

I fake my way through a few days in other people's lives, take on their faces and voices, make believe I can do their jobs, and somehow things end up turning out all right. Or at least better.

But this time I felt like a fraud. Not as if somebody was going to catch me at it—somebody already had. No, it was as if everything I said and did as Philip Larkin was a lie. Worse—a self-serving lie.

Al was right. This Leap was never about a chance of getting home. Things don't work that way, no matter how much I might want them to.

But although this Leap didn't start out being about me, the instant Alia showed up things changed. It's about the two of us now.

And that's all wrong. Philip Larkin helped me make my dream a reality, even though he never knew it. I owe him for that. I have to help him. I have to make sure he lives—

—so he can maybe help bring me home.

Self-serving, and selfish. Some White Knight I am.
No wonder Al isn't speaking to me.

The campground was empty. The Fair was deserted, and what booths had not been taken down were shuttered. No one wanted to miss the epic battle. King Steffan and Queen Elinor arrived with due pomp and settled onto their thrones. The nobles of their court surrounded them on the royal dais. Lesser League members clustered excitedly on the benches. Pennants fluttered, wagers flew thick and fast, and it took the herald three mighty blasts of his horn to quiet everyone down.

Roger was warming up off the field, near a rack of weapons. Sam watched him for a minute, knowing full well that this would be a replay of yesterday morning's joust. He knew no more about swordplay now than he had twenty-four hours ago, his shoulder still twinged, and the sword and chain mail seemed to weigh more than ever. The addition of a shield—*another* ten or twelve pounds of metal to lug around, despite the protection it might offer— made Sam's life just about complete.

His body remembered the moves of various martial arts disciplines, but if he'd ever learned any involving weapons that approximated a sword, he'd forgotten. What he needed to know, he was allowed to remember? Cold comfort, when Roger was eager, willing, and more than capable of ripping his head off if he so chose.

Sam walked around the far end of the field, away from the stands, finding warm-up room directly opposite Roger. As he concentrated on exercises that would stretch shoulders, hamstrings, and back to decent suppleness, he kept his eyes and his mind as unfocused as he could manage. He didn't want to see or think or feel.

The herald blew his trumpet again, attracting Sam's attention. A small parade of mailed knights marched down the center of the field to the dais. They looked like a major league team for some outlandish contact sport being introduced to the assembled stadium fans. Had this been soccer, football, or baseball, Sam would have had a chance.

But although this was, in the end, about winning and losing, it was no game.

He told himself he had to win for Philip's sake. The fundamental honesty inherited with every particle of DNA and inhaled with every breath of Indiana sunshine told him his motives were nowhere near that pure. He wondered dismally why it was so awful of him to want to win for his own sake, too.

"Your Gracious Majesties! My lord, ladies, and gentlemen!" bellowed the herald. "Now begins the last day of the Summer Tourney!"

Sam unsheathed Philip's sword and began hacking at the wind—and at his own feelings—barely reacting when the familiar metallic *whoosh* sounded nearby. So Al was back, was he? The kid who'd slain dragons on the orphanage stairs wouldn't have missed this medieval madness for anything.

Not fair, not fair at all. What was the matter with him? Had Alia shaken his belief so profoundly that he maligned the closest friend he had in the world?

Sam wasn't sure if Al really knew how much he was valued—or why. Through the holes in his memory seeped images of Al in all his various guises. Master manipulator of parsimonious congressional committees; drinking buddy when Sam was discouraged; chief kicker-in-the-ass when Sam was depressed; triumphant partner when a victory was achieved over temperamental technology. A wounded and needful spirit, those first months of their friendship; later, trusting Sam, Al gave and gave with all the generosity of his volatile Italian soul. He was second father and substitute big brother, clever engineer and daredevil fly-boy, courageous warrior and dress-whites admiral and abject worshiper of beautiful women—and somehow, despite their myriad differences in style and personality and experience, Sam's most treasured friend in this life or any other.

In this life, and about a hundred others so far.

But there was more to it now. So much more. When Sam had used Al's cells along with his own in creating Ziggy, he'd been acting on instinct. Research—if he'd bothered to do any—might have confirmed Al the most compatible of the Project personnel, but it had been instinct that bade Sam to test him first. And only. Why save the best for last, when you knew it was standing right in front of you?

Thank God for instinct. In addition to all he'd been before, Al had become lifeline and rescuer; auxiliary memory for a man in unique need of one; counselor, conscience, and occasional gadfly. He was the only constant in this crazy, sometimes frightening, sometimes exhilarating adventure.

Yet if Sam had to define what made Al essential to him right this minute, he would have said it was because over the whole course of Project Quantum Leap, Al had never wavered in his faith that things *would* come out right. Before the Leaps, Al had always believed the money would be found and the problems would be solved and the whole grandiose scheme would work. Now, with Sam bouncing around in Time's gigantic pinball machine, Al believed with everything he was that what he and Sam did was more important than either of them.

Sam needed that faith now. He didn't have much of his own left.

What Alia had said last night was only what Sam had been feeling. *His* doubt, *his* fear and anger and resentment. Bad enough that he hadn't recognized his selfishness while complaining to Al. Worse, listening to Alia say it; worst of all to feel ashamed and scared and to drive away the only person who could help him.

But Al was always there. Whatever his worries and hurts and private concerns, he was always there. The only constant.

"If it please Your Majesties," bawled Herald Owain, "first into the lists, for honor and glory, Sir Neville Sharpsword and the Chevalier de Haut-Roslyn!"

Sam caught sight of Alia, standing to one side of the dais. Midday sun glistened from the crystal headdress, picked out the silver threads shot through her long yellow scarf. She was the perfect medieval damsel, surrounded by the curious and the admiring, smiling as she mimed gentle chagrin at being the center of all this attention.

Sam could hardly bear to look at her.

"Ziggy's come up with some odds, Sam."

He didn't have the courage to look at Al, either. "And?"

"We were right. Win this, and it's a hundred percent that Philip lives. He and Cynthia get together. But the Larkin Capacitor is invented a year late—from our point of view."

"And Roger?"

"If he wins, a hundred percent the gizmo's available when we need it." He didn't have to add, *But Philip dies.*

"That's not what I meant. What happens to Roger?"

"Not sure, but Ziggy postulates a ninety-percent chance that he continues his writing career."

So everybody would live happily ever after—if Sam won the joust.

"As for the odds of your actually beating ol' Rog over there—well, unless one reason you stayed awake last night was for sword practice . . ."

Sam nodded. "That's pretty much what I thought."

"And what *she's* counting on." From the corner of his eye, Sam saw Al direct a look of pure loathing at Alia. "She's enjoying this. She could ruin Philip's life and go picnicking on the wreckage. Sam, you've got to win."

Sir Neville despatched the Chevalier with a supple bit of swordplay that Sam hadn't a hope of emulating. Both young men approached the dais to bow before the royal couple, and Sir Neville collected his accolade. The herald called out another pair of fighters.

"If I win," Sam murmured, "Alia loses. And whatever punishment she faces if she fails, in a way I'll be responsible. Because I'll be the reason for her failure."

"Responsible? Sam, she *chose*—"

"No, Al." He glanced around, hiding a wince at the righteous fury in dark eyes. Doggedly, he went on. "She's trapped in Time. No way out."

"Listen to me. Damn it, *listen*! Forget your stupid rescue complex! It's wasted on her!"

"I thought I was supposed to put people's lives right."

"And *her* only purpose is to make things wrong."

"She feels what I do, Al—tired and angry—we talked about that last night. It scares me that even though what she's sent to do is the opposite of what I'm here to do, we both feel the same things."

Al gave a derisive snort. "So the shiny White Knight suit gets some mud on it every so often! So you're human. So what? I know you, Sam. You don't keep on with this just because the next Leap might take you home. You do it because it's *right*. Because you can't just stand by and not try to help."

The second joust lasted only as long as it took one of the knights to lose his grip on his sword. About three minutes, Sam thought, watching him trudge from the field while his opponent capered to the dais and planted a kiss on a laughing damsel.

"Alia's human, too," Sam argued, finally facing his partner. "You keep saying she's evil, but she's not. She—"

"Are you crazy? Look at her!" Al stabbed a *j'accuse* finger in her direction. "See her for what she is, Sam! She destroys people's lives so she can earn enough points to go home! Alia's responsible for what she is and what she does. Not Lothos. *Alia*. She trapped herself when she made her bargain with whatever sends her through Time—the Devil's bargain. And she knows he'll never keep his side of it."

Another note from the horn was the signal for a dozen children, daughters and sons of League members, to parade in from the far side of the field. Dressed as pages in the royal colors—purple tabards and white hose—they carried what looked like painted yardsticks bearing the flags of various nobles. The eldest child was about ten, the youngest no more than five; her blue unicorn flag was taller than she was. Proud parents pointed out their offspring as everyone applauded. The king and queen greeted each child by name, and handed out sweets as tokens of royal favor.

"Sam . . ." Al's voice was different now, dark and quiet. "Tell me what you remember about your brother."

Startled, Sam frowned. "Tom? What about him?"

"Just tell me."

He thought a minute, then smiled. The procession of flags had reminded him.

"I remember when we all drove to Annapolis for his graduation—commissioning, I guess you call it in the Navy. Mom kept saying she couldn't believe

162

a farm boy like Tom was going to be a sailor."

Appointment to Annapolis and a naval career had always been Tom's dream. That it also eased the financial burden on a farm family desperate to educate a promising daughter and a startlingly brilliant second son hadn't occurred to Sam until later—after he'd seen the cost of tuition and fees in catalogs from M.I.T. and Caltech.

"What else?" Al prompted.

"Dad was so proud I thought he'd bust. He called Tom 'The Admiral' all through dinner that night—" Suddenly he chuckled. "While Katie flirted with Tom's roommate, at only eleven years old!"

Al was watching him through half-hooded eyes. "That's a good memory, Sam. The whole family together like that."

"Why'd you ask?"

"Because on April 8, 1970, your brother Tom died in Vietnam."

Sam felt the world fall away beneath his feet. The grief was both immediate and nearly as old as he was, the agony fresh as a new wound and old as a childhood scar that had never fully healed. It was as if he was learning for the first time of a tragedy he'd been trying to deal with for most of his life.

"No!" he cried. "Tom came back after his tour and—and—" Voice and memory failed him.

Al shook his head. "In the original history, Tom was killed."

"No!"

Inexorably, Al continued, "But you Leaped into that day in 1970. Because of you, Tom didn't die."

"V–Vietnam—"

The river and the jungle and the incredible heat. The welcome breeze of a helicopter's blades. A tough-talking woman photographer—Millie? No, Maggie, that was her name. Bullets screaming past. Slogging through paddies and running as fast as he could because Tom was in danger—*Tom*—

"You changed history, Sam."

Al's voice sliced off the memory before he could reach what his guts yelled at him was the important part, something vital about Maggie the photographer and—*Al*?

"I changed history?" He shook his head in a vain attempt to clear it.

"Where I am, in 1999, Tom's daughter just made him a grandfather."

For a moment Sam simply forgot how to speak. At last he gasped out, "Tom? A *grandfather*?"

"Second time. His son's wife had a little boy last year. Samuel John Beckett." He gave Sam no time to react to—let alone recover from—that one, continuing, "This new baby's a little girl. Olivia Kate McPherson. Tom sent pictures last week. She's got his eyes, and a white streak in her hair just like yours."

Sam's much-vaunted brain had turned to porridge. "Like m-mine?"

Al nodded, his lean face as fiercely watchful as a hunting hawk's, though his tone was carefully casual. "Of course, at two weeks old she's about as prematurely gray as you can get. But Tom says it shows up in the Beckett family every so often."

"We get it from Dad's grandmother," Sam heard himself say, and ran a shaky hand through his own hair. White? When had *that* happened?

And what did it matter? Tom was alive, and he had grandchildren—brand-new lives that had begun after Sam stepped into the Accelerator. Memories he couldn't forget because they'd never been there to remember.

Suddenly, stupidly, he felt like laughing. "My God, I can't believe it! Tom's a grandpa!"

"Yes, he is," Al said. "But if you hadn't been there, Tom would be dead. His kids and their kids never would've been born." The sharp dark eyes claimed and held Sam's stricken gaze. "And that's the bargain *you* make with every Leap, my friend."

The herald's voice split the silence between them like a roll of thunder. "If it please Your Majesties, the challenges of Lord Rannulf and Sir Percival will shortly commence!"

Al gestured to the tourney field. Sam moved like a sleepwalker.

I was wrong, he told himself. *Quantum Leaping isn't a dream I'll wake up from someday. But in a way, Al's wrong, too. It's not a bargain with God. It's an incredible gift.*

Tom is alive—he has children and grandchildren.

But it's not just him. It's all the people I've tried to help. All the lives that came out right instead of wrong.

Something began to well up inside him, compounded of emotions he could barely put names to, filling his mind and heart to bursting. As the herald called out the specifics of each challenge, Sam turned to Al one last time.

"Y'know what?"

Warily: "What?"

Sam could hardly contain the feelings. "Someday, when I wake up in my own bed again and see my own face in the mirror again, my first thought won't be that I'm finally home."

"No?" Al asked, brows arching, still watchful.

"No," Sam replied, grinning from one side of his face to the other. "I'll wonder what's gone wrong in *my* life that I've been sent to put right!"

CHAPTER
FIFTEEN

Donna set the breakfast tray on the mirror table, subtly and deliberately cutting off Philip's view of Sam's face.

"Good morning, Dr. Larkin. I hope you like spinach omelet and sourdough toast."

"Hello, Dr. Alisi. Sounds good. Thanks."

He gave her a tentative smile, and she had to steel herself against a flinch. Sam's smile, the shy and rueful one he'd worn the first time she ever saw him. If it looked anywhere near the same on Philip Larkin's face, Cynthia Mulloy would simply *have* to react to it. Heaven knew Donna had never been able to resist it.

Philip picked up a fork and dug in. "Is Dr. Beckett okay?"

"Fine. How about you?"

"There's still things I can't quite remember, but— I wish you'd let me talk to your computer. That laptop is faster than anything I've ever used, but it still has limitations. If I could get at the mainframe—"

"I'm sorry. If it's any consolation, Ziggy is as frustrated by the rules as you are. She's very eager to talk to you, too. But you understand why that can't happen."

"A person who knows too much about the future can be a danger to the past." Philip chewed, swallowed, and took a swig of cappuccino. "Captain Kirk's Dilemma."

"Capt—? Oh!" She smiled. "Yes, I remember the episode. And, you know, I have a pet theory I'd like to run past you. Do you think there are any scientists of our generation who aren't 'Star Trek' fans?"

Philip grinned and shook his head. "If there are, I don't want to work with 'em. Did they make any more movies after the one where they saved the whales? No, I guess you can't tell me that, either. Or if George Lucas *finally* films the rest of the *Star Wars* movies!"

"Don't hold your breath," Donna advised. She sipped at her own cup of tea. "You know, Dr. Larkin, most people want to know personal things. They ask about their own futures. Family, friends, work. . . ."

Shrugging, he munched a bite of sausage rather than reply.

"You must be curious. Everyone always is."

"You can't tell me, so what's the point of asking?"

It was a sensible attitude. Donna often felt that perhaps they ought to reveal more of the truth to more people. Those who guessed the basics—and the very few who, like Philip, were told—handled it fairly well. She suspected it was a result of this century's fascination with science fiction.

Disclosing enough of the truth to soothe any fears would certainly be kinder than letting people fret themselves into wild speculations. The "alien invaders" scenario—a very popular one with their guests—was definitely attributable to science fiction. Others thought themselves victims of a secret government interrogation squad, the Mafia, the not-so-funny practical jokes of highly creative "friends," international terrorists, and/or stark raving lunacy.

Knowing even the rudiments of Project Quantum Leap probably wouldn't matter. To date, nobody had returned to the past with intact memories. Ziggy devoted an entire memory bank to a zealous search for evidence to the contrary, but no one had gone to the newspapers, written a book, or guested on the talk show circuit. It was the computer's opinion that even if they did remember, they'd be too embarrassed to talk about it—or too apprehensive of being called what they were probably half afraid they were: nut cases.

Donna's theory was that during the passage back, enough of Sam's memories of the Leap were shared so that the person could function, with any glitches chalked up to stress. Thankfully, Ziggy's files had never shown any serious problems cropping up. One or two people had consulted their physicians about blackouts or memory loss, but medical records showed all examinations had turned up clean.

On the other hand, there had been one terrifying Leap when the man in Sam's body had retained much more of Sam than was usual—enough to escape Project Headquarters and lead Al on a desperate chase. The near disaster had taught them that concealment was, after all, the best policy. There was always the chance that Sam would Leap into another Lee Harvey Oswald.

So with regret, because she liked Philip Larkin, Donna said, "No, I can't tell you."

"I figured." He applied butter to sourdough slices with quick, precise movements. Donna smiled to herself. Sam had a tendency to slather things, and leave crumbs in the bed.

"Besides," Philip went on, "Time is pretty much an illusion, when you think about it. We put labels on it, call it *past* or *present* or *future* like it was a verb tense. But those are artificial terms for our convenience. The instant I say *now*, it's already in the past. The *now* I'm in—here, I mean—is really the future as far as I'm concerned. And if you want to get seriously weird about it, doesn't the past become *now* when you're in the process of remembering it?"

Donna felt her brows arch. It really was a pity they couldn't let him converse with Ziggy, who adored this kind of temporal hair splitting.

"And what about seeing into the future?" Philip was saying. "Mainstream science scoffs at it, but the research gets done just the same. Do psychics experience the future as *now*, or as if they're remembering the past?"

Donna thought of Tamlyn, who had experienced the past as the now. Who had Seen past the aura to Sam's own face. Who had loved him, and been loved by him.

170

"Have you read Robert Heinlein's *Time Enough for Love*?" she asked suddenly, certain of the answer.

Philip looked puzzled for a moment, then nodded. "That's just it! All anybody has is *now*, right this minute. No guarantees about tomorrow. And you have to make the most of today because—"

He stopped, as if hearing what he'd just said. Sam's frown creased his face, the lines more pronounced than Donna remembered. The aura changed with time; there'd been several instances when she'd found that between one day and the next, Sam had found privacy enough—and scissors—to make a try at trimming his hair. (Not being able to see himself in a mirror made the operation risky at best.)

Donna's long absence from this room had kept her from gradual notice of small changes. So it was with surprise that she saw the white in his hair was a little thicker and the tiny lines at the corners of his eyes were etched a little deeper.

"I never did that." Philip's weary self-accusation wrung Donna's heart. "I made time for everything except what's important."

"Your work is extremely important." Which was probably the most foolish and patronizing thing she could have said. Worse, it was selfish and self-serving. She kicked herself mentally.

"Sure it is," he muttered. "What about that stupid book? I can't write worth a damn, I know that. If I ever showed the manuscript to Cynthia, she'd know it, too. She'd laugh from now until Christmas."

Reminding herself to tread with more delicacy, Donna said, "I think if a man ever wrote a book with me as the heroine, I'd be flattered."

Philip brought his hand—and the fork—down onto the table with a force that rattled the teacups. "But Cynthia isn't like Alix! The more I wrote, the more I knew the Comte de St. Junien would never fall for someone as intelligent and independent as Alix—the way I wrote her, I mean, as Cynthia—so the book got worse and worse with every word!"

"How do you mean?" Donna asked, pretending not to understand.

He began to pace. *"Subliminal physical inter-facing,"* Donna heard Verbeena say in her mind, watching Sam's long legs carry Philip Larkin from one end of the Waiting Room to the other.

"Cynthia just doesn't *fit* into the Middle Ages!" Back and forth, back and forth, arms flailing and eyes flashing, he talked so fast the words tripped on each other. "I couldn't do it—make her some-one she wasn't, even with another name and—but to be accurate, to make their relationship work—I couldn't make her fit and he wouldn't fall for her the way I wrote her—and to reflect the time as it was—"

"Alix can't be empowered," Donna finished for him. "Liberated," she translated, and he nodded again. "Trying to cram a twentieth-century woman into a twelfth-century society really loused things up, didn't it?"

His mouth opened, but no sound came out for a minute or two. Then he popped up with, "Cynthia doesn't belong in that time—any more than I belong here or Dr. Beckett belongs where *I* am. Was."

"Ought to be," she supplied.

Discovery lit his face. "All we have is *now*—"

"Yes." *When do we get our* now *back, Sam?*

"Dr. Alisi . . . ?"

His voice startled her, but not as much as it might have. Sam would have said *Donna*.

"For a while, with all this technology—and you must know what kind of lure that is for someone like me—and everybody's been so nice to me and all . . . I was thinking maybe . . . I'd like to stay here."

"That isn't possible." And that wasn't the truth.

"I know. But I kind of wished it was." Lean shoulders squared. "But I've changed my mind."

"Have you?"

"Yes. Dr. Beckett shouldn't have had to do for me what I should've done for myself. And I shouldn't be trying to do it in the twelfth century, either."

When you remember the past, it becomes now— well, perhaps. But what about when you create a past? The way Philip did with Lady Alix . . . maybe the way I do by playing Dr. Watson—and the way Sam does with every Leap?

"When I return to *my* now, I'm not just gonna make the most of it. I'm gonna make the *best* of it."

She felt like shouting, *Bravo!* Instead, she hid a smile behind her teacup.

"And whatever I might forget about all this"—he waved a hand at the featureless room—"I hope I remember you."

"Me?" Donna asked, startled.

Philip was blushing. "It's not that you're much like Cynthia—to look at, I mean, she's blond, and shorter, and she's really beautiful, but you're—well, you must know how gorgeous you are."

She fought a blush of her own.

173

"And I don't mean you're not as smart and everything, because I know you are, to be part of all this, but—" He shook his head and laughed nervously. "I better stop, I'm just digging myself deeper! What I meant to say is—" He hauled in a deep breath. "Does it make any sense that the first time I saw you, I felt as if I knew you?"

Flustered, she replied, "It . . . it makes some sense, yes."

"I'm in love with Cynthia," he declared, his face even redder. "The more time I spend with her, the more I talk to her, the more I love her. But—there's things I feel for you, too. I don't understand it, but—"

She took refuge in quoting Ziggy. "A certain degree of merging occurs during any Leap, to a greater or lesser extent depending on the conjunction of neurons and mesons as they pass each other during transfer."

He seemed not to notice the pedantry, going right to the crux of the matter. "You mean I might have some memories right now that aren't mine? Memories that belong to Dr. Beckett?"

All she could do was nod, wondering just what those memories might be—and resisting another blush.

"Oh," Philip said thoughtfully.

Rallying, Donna told him, "Don't worry too much about it. Dr. Beckett often remembers bits and pieces of other people's lives."

"Oh," he repeated. And met her gaze straight on.

Her head spun. Sam's love looking out of Sam's eyes, via Philip Larkin? Feeling completely unequal to this conversation, she made an involuntary move toward the door.

"I'm sorry," Philip said, crestfallen. "I just—do you know? How he feels, I mean. About you. Because *I* sure do." And with that, he turned crimson to Sam's earlobes.

"Yes, I know," she murmured. "He's my husband. I'm his wife."

Philip grinned in delight. "Really? That's great!" Then he caught his breath, and the smile and Sam vanished. "But he's—how long since you've seen him?" He glanced reflexively toward the mirror table and blanched. "Oh my God—you're seeing him right now, aren't you? Except it's not really him."

All at once Philip crossed the chamber in four long strides and grasped her shoulders in his hands.

Residual . . . physical . . . oh, don't do this, Philip, please! Don't touch me the way Sam touches me—

But she couldn't pull away.

"My Capacitor—if that's what's gone wrong with all this, I'll do anything I can to help bring him home, I swear to God I will."

"I'll be back. I swear to God I'll be back. . . ."

His face, Sam's face—the fine lines around his eyes and the faint stubble on his cheeks, the square chin and sharp nose and the yearning curve of his mouth, and the thicker streak of white in his hair that meant years had passed them by . . .

Donna closed her eyes, and something whispered, *Just this once. . . .*

The lips she kissed, just this once and ever-so-lightly in a tiny fragment of *now*, were Sam's.

175

A tremor ran through his bones. She stepped back and he let her go. She looked at him once more.

Not Sam. No, not him at all.

She made herself smile. "Thank you, Philip."

CHAPTER

SIXTEEN

"Why is he *laughing*?" Zoey hissed.

Alia shook her head wordlessly.

From the expression on Roger's face, he was just as baffled as she and Zoey, and angry into the bargain. Forehead corrugated in a mighty frown, he snarled something at Sam as they approached the royal dais. Sam glanced over, surprised—not, Alia thought critically, at Roger's words, but at Roger's mere presence. As if Sam had forgotten he was there—indeed, that any of this even existed. The laughter faded to a smile, but his eyes still danced with some private joke as they threw a glance to the empty air at his left side. No, Alia amended, not empty; the hologram must be there. And in Sam's shining eyes was acknowledgment of a secret only he and his friend Al shared.

In fact, as Sam clapped Roger lightly on the shoulder, he looked as if he'd already won.

"Now?" Zoey asked.

"Not yet," Alia murmured. "Wait."

The two men bowed extravagantly to the royal couple. When the herald beckoned, Alia climbed the short step to stand beside Queen Elinor. She tried to catch Sam's gaze. For all the attention he paid her, she might have been orbiting Mars.

He looked . . . not serene, exactly. Calm?

"Resigned to defeat," Zoey commented silkily.

Alia knew she was wrong. She watched Sam accept an oblong shield and turn smartly on his heel, walking down the field beside Roger, worrying the sight of his face over and over in her mind. Whatever Sam was resigned to—fate? destiny?—it clearly was not defeat. The thought would never enter his head.

" . . . terribly silly of them," the queen was saying. "But I must admit it's rather exciting all the same. Frankly, my lady, I'm wondering why you let this go on."

Alia shrugged, then belatedly recalled her persona and said, "With all respect, Your Majesty, do you think anything could have stopped them?"

The queen gave a rueful smile. "I see your point. Proud as Lucifer, those two."

"How would *she* know?" Zoey asked.

"And stubborn," Alia added, from sure knowledge of Sam Beckett.

Queen Elinor sighed. "Well, you're right, of course. They're angry and nursing a grudge, but they're also accomplished fighters who know the rules. I'm glad they're both using shields today, though."

"At my insistence," said a brown-clad noble seated directly behind the queen. Alia recognized him as the man she'd seen earlier at the sword smith's. "Better they should dent steel than skulls."

The queen half-turned to nod over her shoulder. "Very wise of you, Duncan. But I don't think we need worry overmuch. Neither will be seriously hurt, though I do anticipate quite a few bruises." She chuckled richly. "I trust, Lord Physician, that you have your poultices and potions ready. The stinkier the better, to teach them a lesson!"

"Eh, those two need a shrink, not a surgeon." Lord Duncan snorted, fingering his chain of office—which Alia now saw featured a caduceus pendant. "They're certifiable. And what's all this about a book, anyway, Lady Cyndaria? I thought you joined the League because it gave you an escape from Judith Krantz wanna-bes."

Alia gave him a demure smile. "I know a hot property when I see one, Lord Physician."

"I can't imagine Sir Percival as a closet romance writer," the queen mused. "And as for Lord Rannulf . . . !"

King Steffan hooked a casual knee over the carved arm of his throne. "Yeah, and none of us ever thought we'd see the erstwhile Earl of Stonybrook on 'America's Most Wanted,' either!"

The herald's horn blasted one last time. "Challenge and counter-challenge having been legally issued and legally accepted, Lord Rannulf of the Franks, Sir Percival of York—*begin!*"

After a brief buzz of last-minute wagers, everyone sat forward eagerly as the battle commenced. Zoey paced below the royal dais, hacking away on the handlink, muttering ferociously. Alia ignored her.

Insofar as Alia could tell, both men were holding back, testing each other, reluctant to take

179

the offensive until they'd established each other's physical parameters. Roger had the advantage in height, weight, and reach, but Sam—despite lack of sleep—was the quicker. It was reminiscent of the opening moves of a stately dance, almost a flirtation of swords and shields. As muscles and tempers warmed, Sam began to move in, taking the aggressor's role—which surprised Alia.

"Very nice, very pretty," crooned King Steffan, judicious, as if he were awarding points. "Good tactics, Phil. Make him heft that great heavy shield again and again, and wear out his sword arm at the same time—oh, good stroke!"

"My liege!" admonished the scandalized queen. "You're supposed to be impartial!"

His Majesty gave her a disgusted glance and resumed his color commentary. "Get in under his guard now—oh, bad luck! Come on, Phil, move your ass! That's it! Pivot and swing!"

Every crash of blade on shield brought shouts of approval and groans of sympathy from the crowd. Alia heard a pretty even split of partisanship. She kept her own mouth sealed shut by the simple expedient of biting her lips together. Cynthia's lipstick tasted terrible.

Zoey stepped in front of her, blocking her view. "You'd better give me plenty of warning. Lothos says it might not be instantaneous. There's a possibility that it won't work at all. Alia, darling, do you really know what you're doing?"

She answered with a single scathing glare, and shifted to the right so she could see.

"Come in low now," the king muttered. "Pull back around—ha! Good shot on the shield! Bet that one rattled his teeth!"

Sunlight drenched both chain-mailed knights in glistening heat, striking flashes from shields and plumed helms. Each sword swing became a streaming arc of light, each movement a glitter of sun and silver. Alia supposed it was all rather beautiful, in a barbaric sort of way.

The ground underfoot, already summer-dry and trampled by other jousts, began to exhale little puffs of dirt with every step the two men took. They'd be sweating by now, Alia told herself, needing water, breathing more heavily and inhaling only dry dusty air. Each wore at least forty pounds of metal—chain mail, helmet, sword, and shield—all of it in constant motion as they attacked or defended or absorbed the shock of a blow. She marveled that either of them could stand, let alone fight.

"Alia!"

She shook her head defiantly, anticipating her moment, heart racing as Sam began to falter—but whether she feared for him or feared he would lose too soon, she could not have said.

"Lothos has a lock!"

About bloody time, she thought furiously. Roger drove Sam back with multiple ringing assaults on his shield. Alia strained forward, not knowing enough about swordplay to judge how much trouble Sam was in. But King Steffan's abrupt silence warned her that he was worried.

Suddenly someone cried out as Roger's foot skidded on a patch of relatively fresh grass. His arms

181

windmilled wildly and he lost his balance, going down hard on one hip. Somehow he kept hold of his sword, but the shield flew from his grasp and skidded twenty feet.

Sam gallantly tossed away his own to keep the battle even.

"Nobly done, Sir Percival!" shouted Queen Elinor as the throng roared its approbation of Sam's gesture. Alia decided these people were out of their collective minds—except for the practical Lord Duncan, muttering about X rays and arthroscopic knee surgery, and King Steffan, who flopped back in his throne grumbling, "*Stupidly* done, Phil!"

Sam proved himself as insane as all the rest of these people by reaching a gauntleted hand to Roger, offering to help him up.

"Yes, yes, yes," Alia chanted under her breath.

But Roger slapped the hand away and clambered to his feet, raising the sword once again.

"They're tiring," murmured the queen. "Just trading parries now, trying to get some breath back."

She was right: movements were sluggish, attacks halfhearted and parries slow. The crowd seethed with worry and impatient speculation. Wagers were traded, odds changing constantly. Alia clasped both hands together, Cynthia's rings digging into her fingers, and tasted a drop of coppery blood on her bitten lip.

"Give it a minute," the king said. "They're pacing themselves, that's all. Must be a hundred and ten inside that chain mail—"

"Damn it, Alia!" Zoey exclaimed. "It had better be soon! Lothos can't keep this lock on forever!"

"Ha!" shouted His Majesty. "See? Here we go again!"

The stands rocked with cheers as both knights recovered air and strength enough to come at each other with renewed vigor. Sam advanced, keeping his sword low to spare the muscles of arms and back; Roger scorned the easy way and lifted his blade high and strong. Part of Alia's mind noted each move, realizing that while both were angry, neither was yet desperate enough for an all-out offensive.

There was a strange music to the swords now, or perhaps it was Alia's painfully heightened senses that transmuted each steely clang into a summoning chime that rippled through every nerve. *Soon—please, soon,* she whispered to herself, almost flinching with every blow.

All at once Sam surged close, sliding inside Roger's guard. He grabbed the other man's sword arm with his free hand, struggling to keep the blade immobile. Alia was sure he was telling Roger to stop this insanity now, to stop the fight and talk out their differences before they did each other real damage. Alia's lips twisted tight. Sam could always be counted on to do the rational thing.

What he was about to experience was nowhere near rational.

"Now!" Alia cried.

Queen Elinor, deafened in one ear by the shout, gave a violent start and turned—just as Cynthia keeled over in a dead faint.

Sam heard Her Majesty's distant scream, but what he saw and what he felt dominated his other senses in a rage of disbelief.

One moment Roger was there—tall and massive, handsome face sweat-streaked behind the slotted visor, muscles bulging beneath Sam's glove—

And the next Sam was looking at Alia—slim and supple, her cool pale beauty shimmering inside the silver helm, her wrist bones surely too delicate to support the weight of the sword.

Sam stared thunderstruck into the wild brightness of her eyes.

Her voice was soft and taunting. "I told you, Sam—you don't dare touch anyone again."

CHAPTER
SEVENTEEN

Sam staggered back from Alia as if the touch of her scalded him. She raised the heavy sword in both hands, saluting him—and then brought the blade around in an arc that sought his neck. He lunged out of the way, steel hissing on its way past.

"How the hell'd she do *that*?" Al demanded.

Even if he'd known—which he didn't—Sam had no breath to reply. He was too busy keeping his guard up, in more ways than one.

"Nice work, Zoey!" Alia flung to the empty air nearby, and planted both feet in the trampled grass, marking out her ground. "Give Lothos my compliments!" She swung powerfully at Sam's left thigh, laughing behind the visor.

Sam brought his own blade across and down to block, and the clang of impact reverberated all the way up his arms.

Oddly enough, they were a fairly even match at swordplay. In a moment of sheer insanity, Sam wondered if they'd watched the same Errol Flynn swashbucklers when they were kids. Or maybe the

Star Wars movies—and suddenly he understood something about how to use this massive sword. *Don't try to be an Olympic fencing champion, idiot! Be Luke Skywalker!*

For the moment, however, Darth Vader in the slender form of Alia had the advantage of him: she was fresh and unwinded, and Sam knew she was stronger than she looked. But surely the weight of armor, helmet, and sword would slow her down. It took two very long minutes and a dozen swift and precarious parries for him to realize nothing was going to slow her down short of knocking her out cold. But his shift in attitude about the sword was beginning to pay off. *Treat it like a lightsaber—it's even almost as bright in this sunshine.*

"Get in there and *get* her, Sam!"

The swords met again, sliding against each other until the hilts met and locked like lovers. Sam stared down into glittering blue eyes, laser-bright inside the helm.

"What're you going to do, Alia?" he gasped. "Run me through? You won't kill me. You *can't* kill me. Whatever it is you want, you don't want to die."

The fire in her eyes flared dangerously. "I want exactly what you want, Sam—to be free."

Of everything he had ever heard her say, this one thing he believed without question. He fought to keep the swords steady between them as she pulled and pushed with increasing fury, trying to break his lock.

To be free. They wanted the same thing—but they came at the wanting from totally opposite directions. Or maybe not. Didn't they both want freedom

186

from the loneliness? From the fear that they'd never go home?

"I'm you and you're me, Sam Beckett."

No. Whatever emotions they shared, he and she were not the same.

Alia's cheeks were flushed, her lips thin with effort behind the steel cage of the visor—like cell bars, Sam thought, his mind reeling. How would it be to be trapped as she was trapped, to Leap into someone's life knowing you had to destroy it or face the threat of being yourself destroyed?

She must have seen pity in his face. "You make me sick, you with your self-righteous nobility—"

"Was that for Zoey's benefit?" he panted, forcing her back one step, then another.

He'd guessed correctly; a sudden catch of breath betrayed her. But she rallied instantly, crying out, "Either you kill me or I kill you!"

And in her wild eyes he saw what she really meant: *"You can set me free, Sam—"*

"No! Not that way!" he blurted out, not caring if he betrayed her to Zoey or not. He couldn't let her fall over the edge into the madness swirling in her eyes. "Neither of us has to die, Alia! I can help you, I know I can—"

Hope flashed in her eyes. But then her neck twisted, and she glanced to her right, and terror contorted her features. "Stay out of this! I can take him, damn it!"

"Alia! Don't listen to her! Look at me, let me help you—"

Not this time.

Something he'd read about—and had experienced

187

a few shameful times—came to life in her eyes. Blood lust, battle fever, the near-berserker state when the brain knew nothing but the need to kill. Though perhaps in her it was also the need to die. Whichever, it was too late for Alia; her fragile balance had been lost.

Sam unhooked the hilts and jumped back. The sword was twice as heavy as it had been before and its weight seemed to double with each passing minute. Sweat stung his eyes, matted his hair, slicked his palms inside the leather gauntlets. He had to last long enough to wear her down. Alia wasn't Roger—big-shouldered and skilled, canny with the sword. Sam could win this even if he *wasn't* Luke Skywalker.

"She's right-handed, Sam—that means her guard's weak on the left!"

But she was fighting like a madwoman now, her lips drawn back in a snarl and a low feline growl coming from her throat with every swing of the sword.

"Sam! Look out!"

But he had to win, because if he did, Ziggy's projections about Philip and Cynthia and Roger would come true, and he could Leap out of here.

"Follow up! Damn it, Sam, don't give her time to recover—"

And Alia would find him again. Touch him again.

"That's it! Move in, Sam!"

If he won, she lost. But if *she* won, they were *all* lost.

His aching muscles were suddenly flooded with renewed strength. *"A Jedi feels the Force flowing through him*"—Sam heard the line echo in his head and decided he was becoming hysterical. But whatever it was that had provided the energy, it was his to use. He beat back every blow, taking the attack now for himself. He hacked at her guard until her sword dropped, flat-bladed her on the upper arm, dug the blunt sword tip into the chain mail covering her thigh. She cried out in pain and he flinched with guilt. *I have to do this—I don't have any other choice—Alia, forgive me—*

Failure was staring her in the face. She couldn't win this. She must have known going in that he was stronger. Sam did some frantic mental backtracking, suddenly so astounded that he nearly missed knocking away her sudden swipe at his ribs. God, the sword was so heavy now. His arms and back were so tired. The crowd's roars were a dim and distant buzzing past the thunder of blood in his ears and the harsh wind of his own breathing.

She came at him again, and he parried again, and she gave up a few more feet of dust-choked ground. She must know she couldn't win, that eventually she'd tire. So why was she doing this? Why did she Leap into Roger?

Did she *want* Sam to win?

"Trust in the Force, Luke—"

He let her drive him back step after step. Even as she pressed the attack, her movements telegraphed her bewilderment at his yielding. She drove him across the field toward the wooden fence. Lurching away from the sword slice that damned near hamstrung him, his back slammed hard into the rails. Through a haze of pain he hoped the cracking sound was the wood and not his ribs.

And then she did a bizarre thing. She let him knock her sword away—when he wasn't even trying. She went down on her face, not in an awkward sprawl but in a lunge with both hands outstretched to the saw-horse that propped up more swords, more shields. When she rolled over, she was gripping something he'd never seen the like of before in his life. A wooden handle swirling with blue paint, an iron chain with a spiked ball attached—he gaped at it. Luke had never faced anything like *this*.

Alia was breathing deeply, smiling a terrible smile. The blood lust was gone, replaced by something even more calculating, even more lethal. Perhaps even more insane.

"I bought you a present this morning, Sam."

"Holy shit!" Al yelled. "Look out—that's a morning-star!"

A meaningless identification—until Alia pushed herself to her knees and began to whirl the iron sphere over her head. Golden star-burst spikes blurred as the momentum increased, and then flew like a comet toward his knee.

He barely got out of its way. The spiked ball hit wood with a force that splintered the railing and would have shattered his kneecap.

"She's gonna kill you, Sam!"

"No," he would have said if he'd had breath. What she wanted was for him to believe himself in such mortal danger that the only way to live was to kill.

Alia hefted the blue handle again. The morning-star arced upward and spun, gathering speed. Sam stood between her and the stands, so no one saw

190

clearly that "Roger" was threatening homicide. A few more revolutions, and the morningstar would smash into Sam's left side and probably crush chain mail and ribs clear through to his heart.

Sam flung his sword like a javelin at the chain, and at the same time lashed out a foot, clipping the arm that swung the deadly weapon. Alia shrieked in pain and collapsed to one side. Deprived of momentum, the spiked ball thudded to the ground. Sam dropped immediately and spread-eagled himself across Alia's struggling body.

She groped for the morningstar, eyes crazed with frustration and fear. He knew then that he'd been right: there was no hope for her this time. She had lost her balance on the knife's edge and fallen into the acid black well.

And Sam had pushed her there.

"Stop it, Alia! It's over!" He grappled with her, trying to pin her arms. The leather gauntlets made his hands clumsy. He didn't want to hurt her again, but she had no such qualms; she thrashed beneath him like a wild animal, arms and legs flailing. A fist smashed into his sore ribs, and one side went nearly numb.

She writhed partially out from under him. "You'll have to kill me to stop it, Sam!"

He managed to fling himself onto his back, taking her with him, and pushed off again with a foot. It worked; she was pinned under him again, and he had a grip on one arm.

"That's not the way out!"

"It's the *only* way! If I die, I'm free—because you'll

stay here and never Leap again! That's why I did it, Zoey—"

That was a lie, and he knew it—and hoped to God that Zoey did not. He played his part as he guessed it was supposed to be, wondering if together they could convince Lothos. "Alia, I *can* help you! Listen to me!"

He saw in Alia's suddenly terror-stricken face that it hadn't worked. She was past listening, hearing, understanding: drowning in the knowledge of her failure. Her body arched with frantic strength beneath his. Her fingers scrabbled at his neck, thick gloves clawing beneath the chain mail so she could wrap both hands around his neck and dig her thumbs into his throat.

Air clogged in his lungs. His head spun. From very far away he heard an enraged bellow: "I'm a goddamned *hologram*, Gushie! I *can't* do anything!"

Samuel John Beckett, M.D., knew exactly what was happening to him. The blood supply to his brain was being squeezed off at the carotid arteries; the passage of air was throttled before it got past his trachea; his larynx was bruised and soon would be crushed. He'd never feel it, though; he'd pass out before then.

"Philip!"

From the outside rim of his tunneling vision he saw a blur of yellow that both expanded and receded, then was subsumed in gathering darkness.

Suddenly he could breathe again. It hurt like hell, and when he swallowed reflexively it hurt even worse, but his head was clearing. A sound like an iron temple bell rang in his ears. He waited a moment for his brain cells to flush with blood, then heaved himself to one side, off Alia's limp body.

Cynthia stood over them, blank-faced with shock, the handle of the morningstar gripped in both fists.

Sam tore off his helmet, then Alia's. Her cheeks were splotched with red, slick with sweat. Long lashes fluttered, and Sam exhaled in relief. She was only dazed, semi-conscious at best, but unhurt.

"Get help—hurry!" Sam rasped to Cynthia, cradling Alia's head in one palm, the other hand feeling for the pulse at her throat.

"Philip—"

"Hurry, Cynthia!"

Alia swallowed once, twice, and blinked up at him. "Sam?"

"Here, Alia." He cleared his throat. "I'm here."

"Cynthia's gone for the League doctor, Sam," Al said quietly. Then, reluctantly: "Is Alia all right?"

Yes. And no. The madness had drained from her eyes, leaving only weary resignation. He pulled in a breath that caught painfully in his chest. She knew what awaited her, and was too exhausted even to fear it.

"Stupid," she whispered. "Should've known. I can't even die."

"How could you ever think I'd kill you?"

A corner of her mouth twitched. "That's what Zoey just said. I'm sorry, Sam."

"You don't have to die to be free of Lothos, Alia. There's another way." He stroked sweat-damp hair from her forehead. "There has to be."

"That's something Zoey would *never* say." Her face changed, serious and intent now—and curiously innocent, like a little girl's. "Do you understand? Do you know why, Sam?"

"Yes."

She almost smiled. After a moment she shifted away from him, propping herself on one elbow. She reached up, touching his face briefly. "Sam? Your eyes—they're green."

And he felt the sting of tears in them. "Yours—yours are blue, Alia. And beautiful—"

Incredibly, she was still smiling when her body warped inside the armor and the livid rainbow claimed her, and Lothos took her back.

CHAPTER
EIGHTEEN

The chain mail, once more encasing its rightful owner, clattered as Roger collapsed onto the grass. Sam stared at the man's face—still seeing Alia's. Why had she smiled? Was it because this time she hoped she would pay for her failure with death?

He looked up at Al, questioning mutely.

"Gone," he said, and no more.

Running footsteps warned Sam to get control of himself. Cynthia returned, with various court nobles, all clamoring to know what had happened. Only one, wearing plain brown and a heavy gold chain, did anything to the purpose. He nudged Sam aside and knelt beside the unconscious Roger. Quickly and professionally he checked pulse and pupils.

"Out cold, but he'll wake up in a minute."

"No thanks to you, Lady Cyndaria," accused the herald.

"Now, Harvey," the king began.

"And what exactly was I supposed to do?" she countered. "Let them kill each other?"

"Hold still, you." Fingers startled Sam, probing the bruises and abrasions at his throat. He reared back, pushing the hands away.

"I'm fine," he said.

"You're insane!" Cynthia yelled. The sudden force of her fury actually toppled Sam onto his rump. She was absolutely raving.

"What the *hell* did you think you were doing? Philip, we're not *in* the goddamned fifteenth-century! Fighting over a woman—it's barbaric! I should've clopped you *both* over the head! I couldn't possibly damage brains you don't even have!"

Verbeena Beeks would have called it reaction to stress; Al would have called it temporary gaga. Ziggy would have called it partial systemic breakdown due to overload. Whatever it was, Sam did exactly the wrong thing as far as her ladyship was concerned. He began to laugh.

"Cynthia! Am I ever glad to see you!"

"Don't you *dare* laugh at me, Philip Larkin! And I never want to see *you* again as long as I live!"

But he kept laughing as he pulled her down onto her knees beside him and bear-hugged her— an uncomfortable process, what with his chain mail scraping her bare shoulder and her crystal headdress scraping his cheek. Torn between justifiable rage and stunned amazement that Philip was actually making a move, Cynthia lost all powers of speech.

The herald had no such difficulty. "Highly irregular, Your Majesty—the whole question of the joust— and Lady Cyndaria's illegal interference, using a forbidden weapon—"

196

"Oh, chill out, Harvey." King Steffan waved him aside. "They both acted like total jackasses, but there's no law against *that*. Stupidity isn't a victimless crime, y'know. They're both gonna limp around like Quasimodo for about a week."

"But they broke every rule of chivalry on the books! They actually tried to kill each other!"

"Well, they didn't succeed, did they? Tell you what—I'll bust 'em back to squire second-class and make 'em serve at High Table this Yuletide." When the herald opened his mouth to object further, he was favored with an awful scowl. "We remind you that We Are The King."

"As Your Majesty wills," sighed the herald.

The royal paw clapped him companionably on the back, nearly staggering him. "Good. Glad you see it my way, Harvey. Let's get back to the stands. Damn, I need a beer!"

Sam had meantime released the flustered and blushing Cynthia. He grinned at her. She looked as if she'd purely love to smack him one.

So Sam leaned over and kissed her. It seemed the thing to do; besides, he'd had quite enough of being knocked around for one day, thanks.

"Hot damn!" Al crowed suddenly. "You did it! Brave knight and fair maiden *do* get married! Roger writes four sequels and marries the actress who plays Lady Alix in the movie—I *told* you he was more in love with her than with Cynthia—"

"Fool," Cynthia accused.

Sam hugged her again. Over her shoulder, his gaze fell on the morningstar lying in the grass.

All at once it looked familiar.

But his thread of thought snapped when Roger made feeble swimming motions and moaned. Cynthia helped him sit up, asking anxious questions to which he reiterated his first incomprehensible comment. The doctor looked him over again and departed after seconding Sam's silent diagnosis: gargantuan bewilderment but no real hurts. The morningstar hadn't touched him, of course. Sam figured it must be the shock of transference that had him glassy-eyed.

Sam's gaze strayed back to the morningstar. He'd seen it before—and not just when it was hurtling at him with killing force. Something about the blue-painted wood, the dark chain ending in a gray iron ball studded with golden spikes. . . .

"You two and your *stupid* book!"

This time the interruption was eloquent, and full volume. With her intended audience complete, if not completely functional, Cynthia evidently decided she was more interested in cussing than cuddling. She shoved Sam away from her; he went over on his side again, grimacing.

"Do you know I was actually considering offering an advance? Twenty thousand bucks! For a first novel! Twenty thousand—and you two so set on murdering each other I was sure it'd end up paying for your funerals! Christ on a kayak, I may kill you myself!"

Al listened and admired. "Anybody ever tell you you're just *gorgeous* when you're mad?"

Roger perked up—but not at the threat. "*How* much?"

"Twenty grand." When he made no reply, she

ground her teeth. "All right, thirty. But that's it! Not a penny more!"

Roger gulped, squinting at Sam. "You won the joust. I'm not sure how you did it, but you did."

With no intention of enlightening him, Sam leaned on one elbow and squinted back. "So?"

He cleared his throat. "According to League rules, that means you've been vindicated. You won, so you're right and I'm wrong."

Cynthia threw both hands into the air as if soliciting divine witness to this imbecility.

"So it's all yours," Roger finished.

"Cynthia," Sam said deliberately, "it's Roger's book. He wrote it."

"He did?" Both hands fell to her lap. "Then why did you—all this—the joust and the challenges—" She paused, gathering breath and steam for another tirade. Sam reached up and clapped a hand over her mouth.

"Hush, your ladyship," he grinned. "We're negotiating."

She jerked free and glared at him.

Roger was shaking his head. "You take half, Phil."

"Five percent," Sam countered. "You did the work. And we both know I can't write a grocery list."

"Thirty-five. You did most of the first draft. And it was your idea to put Cynthia in it as Lady Alix."

This took all the wind out of her sails. "It was?"

"Uh-huh," Sam replied.

Wrong thing to admit.

"*You* did that? You turned me into that stupid, simpering, brainless little *twit*?"

"Only in my version," Roger explained. "That's

why Phil's is so cruddy—well, one reason, anyway."
All at once he bristled in defense of the woman he
loved. "And Alix is *not* a twit! She's accurately por-
trayed, and authentic to her era—"

"In the twelfth century, Cynthia, you'd be an
anachronism," Sam supplied helpfully.

"And then some," Roger emphasized, giving Sam
a look that plainly said, *Better you than me, buddy.*
"I only used the way you look. Because the way you
look is perfect. But—" He steeled his jaw, then said
with simple honesty, "But Phil wants you the way
you *are*."

Sam began to understand why the two men had
started out as friends. With luck, they'd end up that
way, too.

"Oh," said Cynthia. She chewed her lip, then burst
out, "Were you planning to tell me about Lady Alix,
Roger, or just let me look like a fool when everybody
else saw it except me?"

"Well . . ." He gulped again. "Actually, if Phil
hadn't said anything last night . . . neither would
I."

"And since he did, you did. *Men!*" she growled,
and Sam saw another flood of creative vitupera-
tion heading their way. But an instant later she
was giving Roger her sweetest smile. "First editorial
decision: no wind chimes. She can knit socks, grow
orchids, or make pistachio baklava for all I care. But
no wind chimes."

"But—that's integral to her character! And the
plot! She—" He took another look at the steel inside
the silken glove, sighed, and submitted meekly. "No
wind chimes."

Sam took advantage of the pause to say again, "Five percent."

"Twenty," Roger replied at once. "Call it an agent's fee."

"An agent's usual percentage is ten," Cynthia pointed out.

Sam nodded. "Okay, ten."

"Fifteen," countered Roger.

Al cleared his throat. "Five percent of thirty grand is a nice chunk of change, Sam. Fifteen hundred bucks would buy a lot of mistletoe. Not that Philip's gonna need it. . . ."

Sam half-choked on laughter. "Okay, okay, fifteen. But I'm taking only ten. We'll use the other five percent to throw the biggest Yuletide party the League has ever seen. Maybe then King Steffan will forgive us."

"I like it!" Roger agreed instantly. "Dinner, a humongous tree, gifts for everybody—"

Sam cast a sideways look at Cynthia. "Mistletoe. . . ."

She arched a brow. "Do you think you'll need it?"

"I definitely like this lady," Al announced.

Roger tugged off his right gauntlet and held out his hand. "Ten percent of the advance to you, five to the League. Shake on it, Phil?"

"Done." Sam removed his own glove. "Y'know, I've got a feeling you're going to do a lot better with that book than anybody thinks. In fact, I see the *New York Times* best-seller list in your future—"

Al gave him a warning look that Sam blithely ignored.

"Two or three sequels—"

"I knew it," said Cynthia. "You hit him on the head too hard, Rog, he's lost it. First he kisses me, now he's gone psychic."

"And a movie deal," Sam went on, "and getting married—"

"If you insist," said Cynthia.

Sam blinked at her. She met him stare for stare.

"My mother always told me to make the most of my opportunities—and a man in a state of temporary insanity sure looks like an opportunity to me."

Al chortled quietly in the background. "Nice work, Sir Percy. Ready to go?"

Roger was climbing gingerly to his feet. "Just don't let her near the weapons rack again. Did she *really* use that thing on me?" He pointed at the morningstar.

"It got your attention," Cynthia retorted. "Even through that thick skull. Besides, I didn't hit you that hard."

"You put a dent in my helmet!"

"So I'll buy you a new one."

Sam fixed on the weapon, his heart suddenly pounding. He knew what was familiar about it now. The wooden handle was painted the same blue as in Philip's drawing; the iron ball was the same gray as the cube; the gold spikes were the same as the squiggly yellow lines.

The whole damned thing was a dead ringer for the Larkin Capacitor.

"Get ready to Leap, Sam."

He shook his head. "Look." He reached for it, arranging it carefully on the grass.

"Look at what?" Cynthia asked.

The Holy Grail.

"The Capacitor," he murmured, almost hypnotized. "When it was whirling around in the air—that's the exact configuration—"

"Can you believe this?" she exclaimed. "Mistletoe to marriage to physics in two minutes flat! I suppose I can learn to live with it."

"If I just keep looking at it. . . ."

Al's confused gaze went from Sam to the morning-star and back again. Then he understood. "If you're looking at it when Philip Leaps in—" The handlink chittered. Al let out a whoop. "It worked, Sam! Patent registered in May 1988—that's a year and a half earlier than before! And get this—he gave it to us for free!"

"Phil? You okay?" Roger crouched on his left, Cynthia on his right.

"Fine." Sam went on staring at the weapon that had nearly killed him. The pattern that might give him back his life. Did everything possess a dual nature, having within it its own opposite?

In the last day, Sam had seen both sides of his own soul.

And Alia's.

"All right, Ziggy, I'm comin'," Al said to the handlink, and Sam glanced up. "No, don't look at me, look at the thingamabob! She says we have an important visitor—and you get one guess who it is," he finished with a grin.

Sam grinned back. He didn't have to guess; he *knew*. Returning his gaze to the morningstar, he felt the familiar tingling begin. He squeezed Cynthia's hand, silently wishing her and Philip well. Another instant, and he would be somewhere else, some other time—

And he thought, as he always did, *And maybe, someday soon . . . home.*

CHAPTER
NINETEEN

She was there when it happened: the sudden tensing of his body, the abrupt lift of his head, the slight puzzled frown, frozen for a split second before the faintest glimmer of blue-white light flickered like St. Elmo's fire and then vanished.

Sam? she thought, as she always did. *Sam, have you come back home to me this time?*

The white-clad body seated on the bench slumped over. Donna and Sammy Jo sprang forward before it could topple. Supporting him between them, they waited for green eyes to focus into sanity.

Sam, Donna thought mindlessly. *Please.*

"It's okay, you're all right, you're safe," murmured Sam's daughter. "Just relax, take it easy. That's it, slow breaths."

Shoulders stiffened, then eased. The women tentatively let go, saw that he could sit upright unaided, and backed off. He cleared his throat, gulped, and looked around.

"Can you tell me your name?" Sammy Jo asked,

her voice soft and quiet, with a hint of a Southern accent.

He divided a perplexed gaze between the two of them. "I'm—I'm Josh," he said slowly, as if not quite sure. "Who're you?"

"My name is Sammy Jo," she replied after a quick compassionate glance for Donna. "This is Dr. Alisi. You're perfectly safe, Josh. Just relax. Can I get you anything? Coffee?"

"Uh—yeah. Please. Sugar, no cream."

As Sammy Jo performed Verbeena's recommended opening of using small social rituals to distract and soothe, Donna moved away and unobtrusively keyed up her wristlink.

Josh sagged slowly back against the wall. One hand came up to comb the hair from his eyes— Sam's gesture.

And then he cried out. "My hand!"

"It's okay, I promise," Sammy Jo said. "Everything's all right."

He was staring at Sam's right hand as if it belonged to a stranger, which—in a manner of speaking—it did. Donna and Sammy Jo watched as with the left hand he touched the right, holding back slightly from the thumb.

When he tried to touch it, the index finger went right through the illusory aura.

Josh began to scream.

Donna spoke urgently into the wristlink. "Ziggy, send Dr. Beeks to the Waiting Room at once. We have another visitor."

A little while later, Josh had been given a sedative and Verbeena had ascertained enough of his history to help Ziggy help Al help Sam. Joshua ben Avram (born Joshua Abramson on April 11, 1949, current age eighteen) had lost his right thumb and the use of his fingers in an accident on the Israeli kibbutz to which his family had emigrated in August of 1965.

Ziggy was not particularly forthcoming, but simple arithmetic meant there was a very good chance that Sam was smack in the middle of the 1967 Six Day War.

Rarely did Sam's Leaps take him out of the United States. There'd been Vietnam, of course, an archaeological dig in Egypt, and one or two others. But Something or Someone evidenced enough kindness to put Sam into situations where he was familiar with the language and culture.

Kindness, or practicality.

Donna walked down the short hall to the control room. She hoped Al was back to tell her what was going on. She hoped young Josh ben Avram wasn't fluent in Hebrew or Yiddish; neither was among Sam's linguistic accomplishments. She hoped Sam could adjust to not using his right hand. She hoped to God he wasn't literally in the middle of the war.

But where else would a young Israeli be at such a time? Josh was of military age. Even if he couldn't fire a rifle or drive a tank, he could be assigned other duties just as essential and just as dangerous. Donna could think of half a dozen right off the top of her head.

Worrying the possibilities over in her mind, she almost missed seeing the tall, lanky, balding man appear around a hall corner up ahead.

"Philip!" Donna exclaimed, surprised. Not only

had no one told her he'd be coming to New Mexico, but not an hour ago she had been talking to his younger self. This time she understood a little of Al's occasional memory gibbers.

"How are you, Donna?" Philip Larkin smiled a greeting, lengthening his strides. They met in a brief hug. "Looking as gorgeous as ever."

"Liar. What are you doing here? Did you bring Cynthia and the kids?"

"They're at Rog and Nadine's place in Pasadena." They started down the corridor to the control room. "Cynthia's got a manuscript she thinks Nadine might want to buy—she's got her own production company now. Rog pulled Disneyland duty." He grinned wickedly. "My three, his twins, and just li'l ol' him to ride herd."

"You're a cruel and vicious man, Philip Larkin, and I don't know why I like you so much." She knew very well, of course. In some ways, he was a lot like Sam, and the pair of *them* got on like a house on fire.

"Where's Sam?" Philip asked.

"I'm just going to find out." She tucked her hand in the crook of his elbow. For a moment she debated about telling him what Sam's last Leap had been. Actually, she didn't have to tell him. In some way he already knew. The first time he'd come to New Mexico, there'd been a look of sudden recognition in his eyes, followed instantly by bewilderment. Though she hadn't understood it then, she did now.

It wasn't often that she got to see firsthand the effect of the changes Sam wrought. Anytime she got to feeling sorry for herself again, she thought, she'd remember the two Philip Larkins.

"Oh, almost forgot," he said. "I'm a day late, but happy birthday."

Donna smiled, and thanked him, and touched the yellow rose pinned in her hair.

"After I checked in with Ziggy, I had a talk with Tina about the hardware," Philip went on. "I think we can do some fine-tuning based on some stuff I've been working on back in New York."

"And the Capacitor?"

"We'll take apart the backup this afternoon and run some tests." He stopped outside the control room door, glanced either way to make sure they were alone, and clasped her shoulders lightly in his palms. "Donna . . . I'll do everything I can figure to do, but I honestly don't know if the problem is in the Capacitor."

He said almost the same thing every time he visited.

She made the customary reply. "If there's anything to be found, Philip, I'm positive you'll find it."

But they both knew by now that the uncontrolled Leaps had little if anything to do with the Morningstar Capacitor.

EPILOGUE

He was himself again.

Suspended in Time; remembering; knowing; watching twinned histories play out all around him like alternate takes of movie film, the wrong ones slithering to the cutting-room floor.

So. You've put it right, Dr. Beckett?

Yes.

And in helping them, helped yourself as well?

Yes.

Paid for the good you did yourself by doing a goodness for them?

Yes.

When will you learn?

He frowned slightly, seeking the voice that emanated from nowhere and everywhere.

What would you say if you were told that you have been theorizing from a faulty assumption?

Faulty—?

You take upon yourself the responsibility for other people's lives—even Alia's.

Yes.

210

Everyone's life but your own.

Shock stilled even the memories.

This is the error.

He didn't understand.

Alia chose her fate. She continues to choose, though she would believe this truth no more than you do.

But—but she was just as trapped as he was.

Precisely. She shares your misapprehension. But the admiral understands.

He traced down the memory, and heard Al say something about a bargain.

The bargain we make is with ourselves. We choose our own destinies, Dr. Beckett. We choose the work we set our minds and hearts to accomplish.

But that couldn't be true. He had no control over his Leaps, no choice, nor even any knowledge of who needed help—so how could he possibly know where and when he was needed?

Knowledge is distinct from information.

Yes, of course. It was the mind/heart dichotomy: what he knew versus what he *knew.*

It can be described in those terms. When you know with the totality of your being that what you do is yours to choose—

Then he could go home?

If you allow it of yourself.

He still didn't understand.

The "White Knight" image appeals to you.

Well . . . yes, he had to admit to that. Al called it his Boy Scout Complex.

Put another way, it is easier for you to be needed than to need. To hope that you are right, rather than to fear that you are wrong. This is your great

211

strength. It is also your great flaw.

But he couldn't change the way he was made. He couldn't stop wanting to help—any more than he could stop wanting to go home.

One day you will. When you believe that choosing to go home is not selfish but selfless. When you know that you are needed at least as much as you need. When you believe that your worth as yourself is at least as great as your worth as other people.

When something went wrong in his own life that he had to put right? When the life he saved might be his own?

As good an interpretation as any . . . from a certain point of view. But not this time, Dr. Beckett.

The memories seeped away, and the light dazzled him, and he Leaped.